Ce

Heroes of the Laboratory and the Workshop

SALZWASSER
VERLAG

Cecilia Lucy Brightwell

Heroes of the Laboratory and the Workshop

Reprint of the original, first published in 1859.

1st Edition 2023 | ISBN: 978-3-37513-424-2

Verlag (Publisher): Salzwasser Verlag GmbH, Zeilweg 44, 60439 Frankfurt, Deutschland
Vertretungsberechtigt (Authorized to represent): E. Roepke, Zeilweg 44, 60439 Frankfurt, Deutschland
Druck (Print): Books on Demand GmbH, In de Tarpen 42, 22848 Norderstedt, Deutschland

HEROES OF THE LABORATORY

AND

THE WORKSHOP.

HEROES

OF

THE LABORATORY

AND THE

WORKSHOP

C. L. BRIGHTWELL

"Toiling, rejoicing, sorrowing,
Onward through life he goes;
Each morning sees some task begun,
Each evening sees it close:
Something attempted, something done,
Has earned a night's repose."—LONGFELLOW.

LONDON
GEORGE ROUTLEDGE AND SONS, LIMITED
BROADWAY, LUDGATE HILL
GLASGOW, MANCHESTER, AND NEW YORK

William Caxton. P. 20.

PREFACE.

SOME months ago, as I was walking in the suburbs of the city in which I live, I met an artisan returning from work, to whom, as he passed, I offered a little book. The man courteously thanked me, and extended his hand to receive the gift. As he did so, I was struck with the strange contrast between his broad, labour-stained palm and my own slight fingers, which nearly touched his, and I experienced a feeling of peculiar and deep interest as I looked upon the working-man, with whom I was thus, for a single instant only, brought in contact.

I would gladly have made him feel that I sympathized with him, for I realized, as I had not before done, how many were the hardships of his lot, while, at the same time, I half envied the feelings of honest independence which of right belong to the hard-working and industrious members of the community, who "earn their bread by the sweat of their brow," in obedience to the Divine command. "I wish I could give him something he would be glad to have, and could talk with him on some subject that would please and interest him," thought I, as I went on my way—

and this wish returned, again and again, to my mind, until at length it resulted in the production of the following pages.

Surely, the history of a working-man's life cannot be without interest for his fellows, especially if it be a true narrative of victorious struggle, and of laborious effort crowned with success. It is true, that but few of this class have given us the personal record of their experience; but there are some who have done so, while we possess trustworthy and instructive memorials respecting many others. They are not, however, readily to be met with, especially in a form suited for general reading. In this little volume the attempt is made to present a few of the more remarkable examples of the kind, in such a manner as to interest those who may here find the life-histories of men of their own class, many of whom acquired wealth and deserved the respect and gratitude of mankind.

In offering this book to working-men, I wish to say a few words with reference to it. There are here given a variety of short notices of men, most of whom laboured in the mechanical arts;—among them, indeed, are four or five names devoted to science, but they may truly be numbered among "working-men;" and they all rose to eminence solely by the force of their own talent and energy, while many of the fruits of their researches were turned to practical account in the service of the industrial arts. So closely indeed is science linked to the arts, that we cannot think of the steam-engine without recalling to mind the philosophic Watt, nor rejoice in the safety of the poor miner without blessing the memory of the illustrious Davy.

Varied as were the circumstances and occupations of the men whose lives are here recorded, they possess in common one characteristic, without which it is certain they could not have distinguished themselves. They were all "diligent in business," and worked with persevering and determined purpose; and hence their ultimate success.

It is indeed true that many, like them, have toiled and striven, who failed to reach the object of their ambition; but these men have not the less truly contributed to the general good, and without their labours the fortunate few who have attained to renown would have been destitute of the means which their skill and diligence have turned to such good account. It is by a series of minute advances—by a constant addition to the stores of experience and invention—that such great results have been ultimately achieved. There is a saying uttered by the Great Teacher of men, which is applicable here:—"Other men laboured, and ye are entered into their labours."

It is a very instructive fact that, during the time of the great religious struggle in France, the working classes took a prominent part as advocates of the Protestant cause; insomuch that a Catholic historian of the day remarks that "the painters, clockmakers, modellers, jewellers, booksellers, printers, and others, who, although in humble trades, have still some exercise for thought, were the first to adopt these new ideas." What a striking testimony to the fact that diligent occupation in the pursuits of business and of trade is no obstruction, but rather a help, to intellectual and spiritual life!

One of the most illustrious of these adherents of religious truth and liberty was Bernard Palissy, a name that deserves to be held dear by working-men in all times. In him we have an illustrious proof that greatness does not depend upon the occupation, but upon the mind. Among the men who have risen from obscurity there is none more admirable and noteworthy than he. As an impressive example of labour, of patience, of perseverance under difficulties, combined with true dignity, piety, and virtue, he must ever be a model to workmen of all professions. His whole career was a blending of religion with the work of common life, and proves "that the man who diligently discharges the duties of the earthly, may not less sedulously—nay, at the same moment,—fulfil those of the heavenly sphere, at once 'diligent in business,' and 'fervent in spirit, serving the Lord.'"

"In all labour there is profit," says the wise man. And experience has set its seal to the truth of this axiom; yet the most precious result, and highest reward of earthly toil, will not be attained unless a man has respect to the approbation of God, by whose appointment it is that secular work is not only a duty, but, in most cases, a necessity.

Deeply convinced of this truth, I cannot take leave

of my readers without exhorting them earnestly to bethink themselves of the Saviour's exhortation,—

> "Labour not for the meat which perisheth, but for that meat which endureth unto everlasting life."

We know that Jesus Christ did not mean, in these words, to bid us cease from working with our hands in the daily callings of life. He has enjoined that as a necessary duty. But He meant, in the abundance of His love to our souls, to bid us so much more earnestly covet spiritual than temporal blessings, as to labour first and most diligently to obtain them. Do we ask—as they of old did—"What shall we do that we might work the works of God?" This is His answer,—"Believe on Him whom He hath sent. Verily, verily, I say unto you, he that believeth on Me hath everlasting life."

NORWICH, 1859.

CONTENTS.

HEROES OF
THE LABORATORY AND THE WORKSHOP.

RICHARD ARKWRIGHT,

THE INVENTOR OF COTTON MACHINERY.

Born 1732—*Died* 1792.

DR. DARWIN, in his "Loves of the Plants," has described poetically the process of cotton-spinning, and in a note to his verse, gives an interesting and graphic account of the machinery employed by the extraordinary man to whose ingenuity this country is so much indebted. "On the river Derwent, near Matlock, in Derbyshire, Sir Richard Arkwright has erected his curious and magnificent machinery for spinning cotton, which had been in vain attempted by many ingenious men before him. The cotton wool is first picked from the pods and seeds by women; it is then carded by *cylindrical cards*, which move against each other with different velocities. It is taken from these by an *iron hand* or *comb*, which has a motion similar to that of scratching, and takes the wool off the cards longitudinally in respect to the fibres or staple, producing a continued line loosely cohering called the *rove* or *roving*. This rove, yet very loosely twisted, is then received or drawn into a *whirling canister*, and is rolled by the centrifugal force in spiral lines within it, being yet too tender for the spindle. It is then passed between two *pairs of rollers*, the second pair, moving faster than the first, elongate the thread with greater rapidity than can be done by hand, and is then twisted on spoles, or bobbins." To this short but comprehensive account of the process of cotton-spinning, is added the information that the great fertility of the cotton plant in these fine flexible threads (while those from hemp, flax, or the bark of the mulberry tree, require a previous putrefaction of the pithy substance, and much mechanical labour, and afterwards bleaching), renders this plant of great importance to the world. The poet prognosticates that since this ingenious machine has not only greatly abbreviated and simplified the labour and art of carding and spinning the cotton wool, but performs both these better than can be done by hand, it is probable that the cloth of this small reed may become the principal clothing of mankind.

"Some are born great—some achieve greatness," says Shakespeare; Richard Arkwright belonged to the latter class. He was born in the year 1732, at Preston, in Lancashire, of parents in a very humble grade of life, and being the youngest of thirteen children, we may readily suppose, owed little to the amount of school learning he received; but he had a ready wit, and contrived to earn a small pittance, with which he hired a cellar and set up a barber's shop, with this sign-board over it—"The Subterranean Barber who shaves for 1d." This novelty took amazingly; and Dick had a great run. The rival barbers of the town were fain, in consequence, to lower their terms, and then he came down to a halfpenny. It is related of him that, on one occasion, he had a cobbler for his customer, with so stubborn a beard that he complained it would cost him a razor, and that the halfpenny would not pay for the wear and tear. But the cobbler persisted he would pay no more than the sign-board charged, and Arkwright good-humouredly expressed himself content. This so pleased the cobbler that he became a firm friend to Arkwright, and introduced him to a man who had invented some machinery, from whom he gained his first ideas on the subject.

It seems beyond doubt that he continued in the trade of a barber till about 1760, when he gave up shaving and commenced business as an itinerant dealer in hair, travelling up and down the country collecting the material, which he afterwards dressed and sold again to the wig-makers, among whom he soon acquired the character of keeping a better article than others in the same line.

It would appear that his first effort in mechanics was an attempt to discover the perpetual motion. It was when inquiring after a person to make him some wheels for a project of this kind that he met with a clockmaker named Kay, who dissuaded him from pursuing his idea, by urging that, in applying the invention to cotton-spinning, he would have a better chance of making a profitable concern. Arkwright, who knew that many inventors of spinning machinery had been utterly ruined, was very doubtful about the matter, and unwilling to incur expense. He and Kay, however, made application to a Mr. Atherton for some pecuniary assistance, to enable them to prosecute their plans. So miserable was the appearance of the former barber that this gentleman refused to have anything to do with the adventure. The two associates persevered, and, having made a model of the machine they had projected, went, in 1768, to Preston, where they made and erected a machine in the dwelling-house attached to the grammar-school of the town. At that time Arkwright was almost in rags; and "being a burgess of Preston" he could not appear to vote during a contested election till the party with whom he sided provided him with a decent suit of clothes.

No sooner was the election over than he quitted Preston and went to Nottingham, being apprehensive that the people of Lancashire would be hostile to an attempt to introduce spinning by machinery. Up to that time the cloths of English manufacture, called "calicoes," which were made in imitation of Indian goods, and so called from Calicut, the place of their production, were formed by a mixture of linen and cotton: the warp was composed of linen and the weft of cotton, it being found impossible, by any means then known, to spin the fibres of cotton into a thread sufficiently strong to be used as warp. The cotton was carded and spun by the women in the weavers' families, and when the demand for these cloths increased greatly, they were unable to prepare sufficient weft to keep the looms employed. The limit to which this species of employment could be carried was soon reached, and if some better method than spinning by the one thread-wheel (which was the only machine known) had not been discovered, the progress of the cotton manufacture must have been stopped, or at best would have been insignificant.

It was natural, this being the state of things, that attempts should be made to contrive some more effective mode; and, in fact, long before this time, spinning by machinery had been thought of by more than one person. A Mr. Wyatt, of Lichfield, invented an apparatus for the purpose so early as 1733, but his undertakings were unsuccessful, and the machines were allowed to perish, no model of them being preserved.

As has been said, Arkwright was apprehensive that his projects would meet with opposition in Lancashire, and he therefore went to Nottingham, where, happily, he took his model to Messrs. Need and Strutt, stocking weavers of that place, the latter of whom was well qualified to judge of the adaptation of the new machinery to its proposed object. He at once was satisfied of its great value, and in 1769 Arkwright obtained his first patent for spinning with rollers, and Need and Strutt became his partners in the manufac turing concerns which it was proposed to carry on under it.

The most important improvement in the apparatus was the application of the two pairs of rollers, the one revolving faster than the other, by means of which the thread was reduced to a great degree of fineness—a most beautiful and effective contrivance, which appears to have been undoubtedly Arkwright's original idea.

A spinning-mill was now erected in Nottingham, worked by horse power, and in 1771 another was built at Cromford, in Derbyshire, to which motion was given by water, being the first works of the kind in this country.

We may now regard our ingenious mechanic as fairly launched on the tide of prosperity, but even after he had succeeded in forming this partnership, a period of five years expired from the first establishment of the works at Cromford before any profit was realized, and a capital of more than £12,000 had been expended. But the greatest troubles he had to encounter were occasioned by the annoying charges brought against him as a plagiarist or pirate of other men's ideas. He was even denied altogether the merit of being an original inventor, and a series of expensive and wearisome trials were instituted for the purpose of invalidating his patents.

There would be little interest in relating the particulars of these charges. Suffice it to say that, while some of them were undoubtedly fallacious, and others doubtfully supported, the several inventions which his patents embraced would probably, but for him, have been of no avail. None but himself had the courage and determination to face the fatigues, difficulties, and dangers that lay in the way of achieving such great results—and over them all he, at last, completely triumphed.

To him alone belongs also the merit of having combined the various portions of the machinery with admirable skill and judgment, and of having been the first to turn it to practical use on anything like an extensive scale.

When he started on his career, he was poor, friendless, and utterly unknown; and his example stands out as a most marvellous proof of what a resolute heart, combined with ingenuity and perseverance, may accomplish. This—as Mr. Coleridge has well said—is the grand lesson which the history of Arkwright's life is fitted to teach us;—to give ourselves wholly to one object, and never to despair of reaching it. It was the character of the man to devote his whole heart and faculties to whatever he engaged in, and this was the cause of his success.

At length the undertaking, so long a source of anxiety and expense, began to be remunerative, and from that time wealth continued to flow in abundantly to the proprietors. The works were greatly extended, and several new ones formed; and this tide of prosperity continued, notwithstanding the adverse decisions of the courts in regard to his patents. For several years the market prices of cotton twist were fixed by Arkwright, all other spinners conforming to his scale. The increase of the cotton trade was the increase of his property, and in pursuing his own fortune, he became the source of riches to others—a public benefactor, and a friend to the poor. He had not the tastes and pursuits of a man of education and refinement; but with praiseworthy constancy he adhered to business, and found in it his pleasure. Even to the close of his life the management of his different factories was his daily occupation: into every department of these great establishments he at once introduced plans of arrangement and systematic order, which have since been universally adopted, and have remained, after long experience, unaltered and unimproved to the present time. Surely there could not be given a stronger proof of the originality and comprehensiveness of mind of this remarkable man.

Mr. Arkwright served the office of High Sheriff of the county of Derby in 1786, and on occasion of presenting an address, was knighted by the hand of George III. He died in the month of August, 1792, at his house at Cromford, in the sixtieth year of his age, leaving behind him a fortune estimated at little short of half a million sterling.

Surely his country owes him a debt of gratitude, as one whose skilful industry has exerted a most powerful influence upon the condition of her manufacturing interests.

CLAUDE LOUIS BERTHOLLET,

THE CHEMIST.

Born 1748—*Died* 1822.

AMONG the illustrious men renowned for their devotedness to the cause of science, and its application to the practical purposes of civil and social advantage, M. Berthollet holds a high and honourable place. His name has long been known in every part of Europe, and will ever rank among those of the distinguished chemists of the nineteenth century. He was born at Taloire, in Savoy, in 1748, and was connected, on his mother's side, with one of the noble families of that country. Although far from being wealthy, his parents bestowed on him an excellent education. Yielding to his early predilection for science, he studied medicine; and after taking his degree as M.D. at the University of Turin, he went to Paris, where he devoted himself with great diligence to the study of chemistry. But his researches, however important to his subsequent career, were not at first remunerative, in the sense of procuring him money; and he must have been compelled to quit Paris for want of means, had he not found in Tronchin, a pupil of the great Boerhaave, who was then high in popularity as a physician, a kind and generous friend. Both were Savoyards, descended from families originally banished from

France by the great wars of religion. Here was a bond of union ; and Tronchin was struck at first sight with the appearance and address of young Berthollet, and before long he became fondly attached to him ; and so efficacious was his patronage, that he succeeded in getting him nominated one of the physicians of the Duke of Orleans, the uncle of the reigning sovereign.

He soon became known for his chemical knowledge and skill, and for the original and independent mind which he brought to bear upon the science to which he devoted all his powers, and in whose interests he expended his whole existence. Prior to the outbreak of the French Revolution, the improvements which Berthollet introduced, by his scientific discoveries and indefatigable researches, into the arts of bleaching and dyeing, secured for him universal gratitude and applause. One of his most important discoveries was that of the application of oxy-muriatic acid to the purposes of bleaching. Cloth, when first taken from the loom, bears a faint colour, which must be made to disappear entirely before the material can be dyed. This was formerly effected by bleaching on the grass and repeated washings—a very long and inconvenient process, and one requiring great extent of ground. Berthollet substituted the chemical process now in general use (and which has also been applied to the preparation of paper), which is now brought to a degree of perfection never attained under the old methods.

Great saving of labour, time, and expense, immense

tracts of waste land restored to cultivation, the preservation of the cloth from the injury by friction, and the purity of the whiteness in the bleach, were the results of this valuable discovery. The only personal advantage Berthollet ever derived from it was a present of a bale of cotton-stuffs bleached by his process, which was sent to him by an English manufacturer. It is not improbable that this was the celebrated Mr. Watt, who immediately saw the importance of the discovery, and actually applied it in whitening five hundred pieces of cloth. With noble disinterestedness, Berthollet refused to sell or monopolize his invention, which would infallibly, in the course of a few years, have enormously enriched him. His desire was that the benefit should be diffused as widely as possible; and without loss of time he communicated his experiments, and subsequently published them in his work entitled "Description of the Bleaching of Cloths." Berthollet united great energy of character to his remarkable scientific capacity. M. Pariset, in his eulogium on this great chemist, relates an anecdote which deserves to be perpetuated. During the bloody period of the Revolution, when the self-constituted tyrants of France demanded an implicit obedience, under penalty of death, Berthollet was commanded to examine some casks of brandy suspected of being poisoned. Finding in them no injurious substance, he sent in a favourable report; but this did not satisfy the accusers, who were probably desirous of ruining the unfortunate merchant, that they might confiscate his goods. Accordingly, Berthollet was sent for and interrogated. "Are you sure of what you tell us?" they asked in ferocious accents. "Perfectly sure," was the calm reply. "Would you be willing to make the experiment upon yourself?" He unhesitatingly filled a glass and drank it off. "You are very bold," exclaimed one. "Less so now than when I sent in my report," was the intrepid reply.

Subsequently to the Revolution, when France was cut off from the usual resources of foreign supply, he came forward with other eminent men to remedy the deficiency by the appliances of skill and science. In the organization of the celebrated Institute of France, which comprehended all the men of talent in the capital, Berthollet took the lead, and long laboured, with the most active assiduity, to promote its interests.

After the subjugation of Italy by the French arms Berthollet and Monge, the celebrated geometrician, were appointed deputies by the Directory, to select those objects of the arts and sciences, which ought to be transferred to Paris. In the execution of this task Berthollet came under the notice of Napoleon, who, struck with his genius and practical talent, formed a high opinion of him, and when he subsequently transported a French army to Egypt, which it was hoped would prove a valuable colony to France, he induced Berthollet, with a band of savants, to accompany him. During this campaign he rendered himself remarkable by his personal intrepidity, his humanity, his scientific investigations, and by the respect which the Commander-in-chief paid to his merits and usefulness. Many traits, illustrative of the courage and energy of this remarkable man, are preserved with reference to this expedition. In the desert, and among the wild Mamelukes, he was ever foremost in acts of daring, and by his example, he animated the courage and gaiety of the soldiers. After the disastrous retreat from St. Jean d'Acre, he gave up his carriage to the wounded generals, and traversed on foot twenty leagues of desert, as though it had been a mere excursion. In the pursuit of his scientific researches he did not hesitate to encounter all sorts of dangers. It would have been well if his courage had sprung from a higher source than mere animal spirits; but, like so many of his companions and the men of his age, he regarded not God, and practically set aside His authority. On one occasion, when fired on by some Mamelukes, as he passed in an open boat along the Nile, he was observed to fill his pockets with stones; and being asked what he was about, he replied:—"Making ready to sink; so that I may not be mutilated by these rascals!"

On his return to France, in 1799, he was nominated a senator, and received the distinction of grand officer of the Legion of Honour. He was afterwards provided with the rich senatorie of Montpellier. All this liberality on the part of his Imperial master did not, however, suffice to meet the multiplied demands upon him. His numerous experiments, made on such a large scale, his constant labours for the improvement of the arts, and the maintenance of a vast laboratory, which he kept always open to his friends and to strangers, and above all, to the numerous pupils whom he delighted to see studying under his auspices the most delicate processes of chemical science,—all this exhausted his means, and he was obliged to reduce his personal expenses, to sell his horses, and to withdraw from court. But Napoleon, who entertained for him a high regard, and called him his chemist, summoned him to the Tuileries, and after reproaching him for not making known his circumstances, gave him a munificent present, which he repaid by fresh discoveries and new services rendered to science. Not long after he returned from Egypt, M. Berthollet took up his residence at Arcueil, a village about three miles from Paris, where he pursued, in peaceful seclusion, those fine researches which adorned the close of his career. There he established a society for the advancement of the sciences he loved, and surrounded by men of like pursuits and kindred talent, reaped the best rewards which earth can give, in the friendship and esteem of his compeers.

Alas! this tranquillity was abruptly and for ever destroyed, in consequence of the dreadful event we are about to relate. He had an only son of the most promising talents, who had already co-operated with his father in scientific researches and publications, and whose abilities and character had excited the most sanguine expectations of his friends. This unhappy youth was seized with despondency, which produced fearful results. Notwithstanding the celebrity of his father, the affection of his mother, and the honours which appeared to await him, existence became a burden too insupportable for him to endure. Destitute of the consolations of religious hope, and without holy principle, he had recourse to self-destruction, and the horrible crime was perpetrated with almost unparalleled coolness and desperate deliberation. He retired to a small room, fastened the door, closed up every aperture which could admit the external air, and placing his writing materials and a stop watch upon his table, lighted a brazier of charcoal before him. As the process of suffocation went on, he continued to note down the sensations he experienced, and persevered in describing the increase of his suffering until his hand-writing became illegible, and he ceased to breathe! Such a fearful catastrophe recalls to our mind those solemn words, "Without God and without hope, in the world."

The most prosperous career, the most brilliant talents, even the exercise of the most amiable and beneficent virtues, cannot shield a man from suffering in his own person and in those he loves, the consequences of forgetting the paramount claims of Him by whom all his powers have been imparted, and to whom his life is due. Although M. Berthollet survived some years this overwhelming stroke, he never recovered his equanimity. A profound melancholy and disquiet were written indelibly in his countenance, yet still, with characteristic fortitude, and in the spirit of that philosophy which was all the consolation he knew, he continued to discharge the duties that claimed his attention, and bore, without complaint, a long and suffering illness. At length he expired, in 1822, at the advanced age of 74. Oh! that he had been a Christian; then would he indeed have been of "the highest style of man."

JAMES BRINDLEY,

THE ORIGINATOR OF CANAL NAVIGATION.

Born 1716—*Died* 1772.

"He is as plain a looking man as one of the boors of the Peak, or one of his own carters; but, when he speaks, all ears listen, and every mind is filled with wonder at the things he pronounces to be practicable."

SUCH is the account given of this remarkable man, a person of extraordinary genius for mechanical invention, and who attained distinction by his skill in planning and conducting inland navigation. His history is a most instructive one, and well calculated to encourage those who find themselves under the greatest disadvantages in early life.

He was born at Tunstead, in the county of Derby, in the year 1716, of parents who possessed a small freehold, the income of which was unhappily dissipated by his father, who utterly neglected the care of his son, so that he was deprived of the advantages of even a common education. This disgraceful conduct reduced the family to want, and James, until he was seventeen years old, was employed as a farmer's lad, and had no better chance than the children of the poor cottagers around him.

At that age the lad bound himself apprentice to a wheelwright named Bennet, who lived near Macclesfield, in Cheshire. This man, being generally occupied in distant parts of the country, bestowed but little instruction upon young Brindley, who was left much to his own resources; and these circumstances, so far from being adverse to his improvement, seem only to have called forth more strongly the peculiar qualities of his mind. He was gifted naturally with great inventive faculties, and even in the early part of his apprenticeship frequently astonished his master by the clever improvements which he suggested; and when left to manage the business without any instructions, he gave so much satisfaction to the millers who employed him, that before long he was consulted in preference to Bennet, or any other workman.

Faithful in his situation as servant (would that all apprentices had the same high principle to rule their conduct!) he was anxious to uphold the credit of his employer. On one occasion, he had an excellent opportunity for exerting himself on this behalf. It chanced that Bennet was employed in preparing some machinery of a new description in a certain paper-mill, but a rumour was circulated that he did not know what he was about, and would be unable to execute his contract. This report coming to the ear of Brindley, as soon as he had finished his week's work, and without saying anything of his intention, he set off for the mill, and took a careful survey of the works. After a walk of fifty miles, the energetic youth reached home in time to recommence work on Monday morning: he had marked with discerning eye the points in which his master's work was defective, and enabled him to correct them. The result was that Bennet's engagement was satisfactorily fulfilled. Before his apprenticeship had expired, when, through age and infirmities, his master became unable to work, this admirable young man carried on the business for him with reputation, and provided a comfortable subsistence for the old man and his family.

Brindley afterwards engaged in the millwright business on his own account; but he did not confine himself to the making of mill-machinery. In 1752, he contrived an improved engine for draining some coal-pits at Clifton, in Lancashire, which was set in motion by a wheel 30 feet below the surface, and the water for turning which was conveyed from the Irwell by a subterraneous tunnel 600 yards long. In a short time the fame of his inventions spread far beyond his own neighbourhood; and, in 1755, a gentleman of London engaged him to execute a portion of the machinery for a silk-mill at Congleton. The construction of the more complex parts was at first intrusted to another individual, who, assuming airs of superiority, treated Brindley as a common mechanic, and refused to shew him his general designs, until, as he was found incapable of performing his portion of the work, it became necessary to take the advice of Brindley, who offered to complete the whole of the machinery in his own way; and the proprietors, convinced of his integrity and talents, allowed him to do so. The ability with which he accomplished this undertaking raised his reputation still higher.

Shortly after this time he was consulted by the Duke of Bridgewater, on the practicability of constructing a canal from Worsley to Manchester. His introduction to that nobleman was the turning incident of his life, and led to the application of his talents to the promotion of artificial navigation, in which his mechanical genius found ample scope for exercise, and which proved the commencement of a sort of era in the industrial history of our country.

The duke possessed an estate at Worsley, about seven miles from Manchester, which contained a rich bed of coal, but it was comparatively of little value, in consequence of the heavy expense of land carriage. A great variety of expedients were suggested for overcoming this difficulty, and at length the idea of constructing a navigable canal was adopted by the duke, who, with considerable difficulty, obtained an Act of Parliament for the purpose. He was most fortunate in selecting Brindley as his engineer, for he found in him a man whose genius was unfettered by commonplace rules, and one exactly fitted to carry into execution a project, not only perfectly novel at that time, but which, even in the present day, would demand the highest practical science. Nor was the engineer less happy in his noble patron, who firmly supported him in his bold and original views, and was not deterred by the difficulty and magnitude of the plans he offered.

Having completed the canal as far as Barton, where the Irwell is navigable for large vessels, he proposed to carry it over that river to an aqueduct thirty-nine feet above the surface of the water. An eminent engineer, who was consulted on the occasion, ridiculed the attempt. "I have often heard," said he, "of castles in the air, but never before was shown where one was to be erected." The duke, however, was not discouraged, but, confiding in the judgment of Brindley, empowered him to prosecute the work, and in about ten months the aqueduct was completed.

The canal from Worsley to Manchester being finished, the scheme was then extended to Liverpool, and the whole grand undertaking was accomplished. All the ingenuity and resources of our engineer were called into action in the course of this enterprise, and he proved equal to every emergency; so that where the greatest difficulties stood in the way, his talent was displayed with the greatest effect. Nor was it only in expedients for overcoming obstacles that his skill was shown; he made use of many new and ingenious contrivances for conducting the work with the utmost economy.

The success of this undertaking was the means of fully awakening public attention to the advantages of canals. It is highly probable that, had a man of inferior ability engaged in the work, it would have proved a failure, and the improvement of our inland navigation would most likely have been delayed till some years later. The Duke of Bridgewater's canal was referred to at that time by the projectors of similar undertakings, in the same way as the Manchester and Liverpool railway has been recently quoted in prospect of any new railroad. It is a striking fact that, within forty-two years after the duke's canal was opened, application had been made to Parliament for 165 Acts for cutting canals in Great Britain, at an expense of £13,000,000.

In 1766 the Trent and Mersey Canal was commenced under Brindley's superintendence. It was called by him "The Grand Trunk Navigation," owing to the probability, from its great importance, of many other canals being made to join it. It was carried on as long as he lived, and after his death successfully completed by his brother-in-law.

He next designed a canal for the purpose of connecting the Grand Trunk with the Severn, and also planned that of Coventry, but did not superintend its execution. Some short time before his death he began the Oxford canal, which connects the Thames with the Grand Trunk through the Coventry canal. These works opened an internal water communication between the Thames, the Humber, the Severn, and the Mersey, and united the great ports of London, Liverpool, Bristol, and Hull, by canals which passed through the richest and most industrious districts of England.

Mr. Brindley's last public undertaking was the canal from Chesterfield to the river Trent at Stock with. He surveyed and planned the whole, and executed some miles of the navigation, which was finished by his brother-in-law in 1777. Such was the established reputation to which he had now attained, that few similar works were executed without consulting him.

Of the numerous and truly astonishing works accomplished by this remarkable man, we have only been able to mention some of the principal. Many ingenious schemes and inventions were originated by him, of which Phillips, in his "History of Inland Navigation," gives some particulars; and he was well qualified to do this, since he states he had himself been in the "employ of the great Brindley."

We are assured that his designs were drawn from the resources of his own mind alone. When difficulties occurred in the execution of any of his works, he had no recourse to books or the labours of other persons. On such occasions he generally retired to bed,* where he would remain, one, two, or three days, when he would get up and proceed to execute the designs he had made, without any drawing or model, which he never used, except for the satisfaction of his employers. He read little, and wrote less, his want of education compelling him to cultivate, in an extraordinary degree, the powers of memory; and so tenacious did that faculty become, that he could remember and execute all the parts of the most complex machine, provided he had time, in his previous survey, to settle in his mind the several departments

* Dr. Wallis, who was eminently distinguished for the tenaciousness of his memory, so that he could extract the cube-root of any number to one hundred places of figures in his mind, used frequently to avail himself for this purpose, of the same seclusion.

and their relations to each other. In his calculations of the powers of any machine, he performed the requisite operation by a mental process, in a manner which none knew but himself, and which, perhaps, he was not able to communicate to others; and after certain intervals of consideration, he noted down the result in figures, and then proceeded to operate upon that result, until at length the complete solution was obtained, which was generally right.

It was said by those who knew him best, that his conversation on occasions of importance, and among his intimate friends, was highly instructive and entertaining, being enlivened by his own peculiar genius. It is certain no man was more entirely free from jealous feelings. His incessant attention to important and absorbing objects made him indifferent to any of the usual amusements and pastimes commonly had recourse to for recreation. It is said that he was once prevailed on, when in London, to see a play, but he found his ideas so much disturbed, and his mind rendered unfit for business, that he would, on no account, go to another. All his powers were devoted to business matters, and such was the enthusiasm with which he engaged in his schemes of inland navigation, that he is reported, when asked, before a Committee of the House of Commons, for what purpose he supposed rivers were created, to have replied, after some deliberation, "to feed navigable canals."

In his private character he was much respected; and being most benevolent and patriotic in spirit, this disposition gave energy to all his pursuits. Such a man could not but reflect with satisfaction that his labour had done incalculable service in the promotion of the public prosperity. He must have thought with exquisite satisfaction of the thousands of poor people who enjoyed the results of that great work which had brought to them the blessing of cheap fuel; for before the construction of the Duke of Bridgewater's canal, coals were retailed to the poor at Manchester at 7*d.* per cwt., while after its completion they were reduced to 3½*d.*, and six score were given to the cwt.

The multiplicity of his engagements, and the constant and close attention which he bestowed on them, were very prejudicial to his health and shortened his life; for some years he suffered occasionally from attacks of low fever, which at length terminated his useful and honourable career. He died at Turnhurst, in Staffordshire, in the month of September, 1772, being in the fifty-sixth year of his age.

The principal events in the life of this truly original man were primarily gathered from materials furnished by his brother-in-law and other friends, who spoke highly of "the integrity of his character, his devotion to the public interests, and the vast compass of his understanding, which seemed to have an affinity for all great objects, and likewise for many noble and beneficent designs, which the multiplicity of his engagements and the shortness of his life prevented him from bringing to maturity."

WILLIAM CAXTON,

THE FIRST ENGLISH PRINTER.

Born 1412—*Died* 1491.

WHAT does not England owe to the glorious art of printing? All honour, then, to the man who first introduced it into our country, and firmly established it there. It was the zeal, perseverance, and patriotic spirit of *William Caxton* that effected this; and although we know but few of the events of his life, yet what we do know serves to confirm the lesson which all experience teaches—that close attention, and unwearied industry and labour, are necessary to success in the achievement of anything worthy the doing, and by which we may benefit our fellowmen and deserve their gratitude.*

We have asked, what does England owe to this inestimable art? But, in truth, we can little realize the condition of our country prior to its invention. How vague and imperfect is the idea we can form of what the state and amount of knowledge must have been when all the books in the world were written out by hand!

Of books and booksellers in the early part of "the

* "To this art," says Dr. Knox, "we owe the Reformation." The monks were its inveterate opposers, and the Vicar of Croydon, as if he had foreseen the Reformation which it subsequently effected, truly enough exclaimed, in a sermon preached by him at St. Paul's Cross: "We must root out printing, or printing will root us out!"

dark ages" but little is known. It is probable that, during many centuries, there was no mode of procuring a book but by borrowing it, and employing a writer to transcribe it. We are told, however, that books, as well as other articles, were occasionally sold in the porches of the churches—where law-meetings were held and money paid, that its payment might be attested, if needful, by some of the persons there assembled. We may suppose that, for the same reason, books were sold there.

We learn from history that many individuals, even in the dark ages, spent much of their time and money in endeavouring to discover and procure MSS. The labours of these lovers of literature were doubtless instrumental in producing such a state of inquiry as prepared men's minds for the invention of printing; and, in the course of ages, the great mass of the people began to be more awake to the importance of knowledge. Above all, the great events which took place in the moral and religious world of Europe, at the period when this discovery was made, prepared the way for a due appreciation of the vast blessing Divine Providence was about to bestow. As early as the commencement of the fourteenth century playing-cards were known and used in Germany: at first they were painted, but towards the close of the century a method was discovered of printing them by blocks. This was the first step towards printing. There were two or three other preliminary steps, but it was not till about the year 1438 that John Guttemberg, of Mayence, first discovered and practised the art of printing with moveable types. After long and vexatious difficulties, he succeeded in entering into partnership with John Fust; and by them was published the celebrated first edition of the Bible from metal types, remarkable for the texture of the paper, the excellence of the execution, and the blackness and lustre of the ink. It is supposed to have been printed in 1455. The expense of printing it gave rise to a lawsuit between Guttemberg and Fust. The very first book with a certain date was an almanack, published by Guttemberg, in 1456. In the year 1462, the city of Mayence was assailed and taken by the Elector Adolphus, and in the troubles that followed, the partners suffered much, and their workmen dispersing themselves, the art of printing was by their means spread over Europe.

We proceed to give a short account of the life of William Caxton. He was born, as he himself tells us, in the Weald of Kent. Of the origin, rank and employment of his parents we are ignorant; but that they performed their duty to their son, we are thus informed:—"I am bounden," he says, "to pray for my father and mother's souls, that in my youth sent me to school, by which, by the sufferance of God, I get my living, I hope truly." This was no small praise,—for in those days, when learning was at a much lower ebb in England than in most of the continental states of Europe, the simplest and most common education was too often neglected. At the age of fifteen or sixteen, young Caxton was apprenticed to William Large, a considerable mercer of the city of London, who was afterwards sheriff and mayor.* Having served his apprenticeship, Caxton took up his freedom in the Mercers' Company, and became "a citizen of London town."

That he had conducted himself during the time of his service to the satisfaction of his master is proved from the circumstance that in his will, in 1441, he left to William Caxton a legacy of 20 marks (13*l.* 6*s.* 8*d.*), a considerable sum in those days, when the usual price of wheat was 5*s.* 4*d.* a quarter, malt 4*s.* a quarter, and a pair of plough-oxen could be purchased for about 23*s.* In the year after he received this legacy he went into the Low Countries. How he had been employed in the interim, from the expiration of his apprenticeship till this period, we know not, but probably in the management of mercantile affairs; and it is conjectured that he left England either as an agent for some other merchant, or on his own account. He continued for some considerable time in the Low Countries, which were then the great mart of Europe, where was carried on the trade of the produce and manufactures of most parts of the world. Hence their friendship and alliance were eagerly sought by the neighbouring powers, and treaties of commerce between them and England were frequently made and broken. It required considerable knowledge in mercantile affairs to conduct these alliances, and consequently merchants were not un-

* At that time the term *mercer* had an extensive application, being given to general merchants trading in all sorts of goods.

commonly employed on such occasions. The character and experience of Caxton as a man of business, and his long residence abroad, seem to have pointed him out as a fit person for this embassy; and we accordingly find him appointed, in 1464, as an ambassador, "to continue and confirm a treaty of commerce with Philip duke of Burgundy." This prince was one of the most powerful rulers in that part of Europe, and his court one of the most polished. His taste for literature and chivalry made him a patron of the liberal arts; and it was natural that Caxton should acquire in such a school much information, which he afterwards turned to excellent account; in fact, he seems to have mastered the French language, and gained some acquaintance with the Flemish or Dutch: above all, he imbibed his passion for learning and romance, and made himself master of the art of printing "at great charge and dispense," as he tells us. His intimacy with Raoul le Fevre, chaplain to the duke, and with another ecclesiastic of the court, probably much influenced the course of his studies. The former was the author of two works which were afterwards translated and printed by Caxton, who became a permanent resident at the Dutch court, on occasion of the marriage of Charles, son and successor of the Duke of Burgundy, with the Princess Margaret, sister of our Edward IV. This event took place in June, 1468, and Caxton was appointed to a situation in the household of the duchess soon after her arrival in the Netherlands.

We have no means of ascertaining what his duties

were in this new capacity, but it is evident they were not urgent, and left him plenty of time on his hands. He says, with much *naïveté*, "I had now no great charge or occupation, and wishing to eschew sloth and idleness—which is mother and nourisher of vices—having good leisure, being at Cologne, I set about finishing the translation of the 'Histories of Troy'—(written by R. le Fevre). When, however, I remembered my simpleness and my imperfection in French and English, I fell into despair, and for two years after laboured no more in this work." The translation, however, was eventually resumed, by command of the duchess, who, learning from the author the history of the attempt and its renunciation, desired him "to continue and make an end of the residue," which command he "durst not disobey." He mentions, in his preface to the volume, that "his eyes were dimmed with over-much looking on the white paper, that his courage was not so ready to labour as it had been, and that age was creeping on him daily, and enfeebling all his body; and finally, that he had learnt and practised at great charge and dispense to ordain the said book in print, and not written with pen and ink, as other books be."

It thus appears that he had acquired the art of printing; but by what means he became acquainted with it, cannot be discovered. It is evident, from his types, that he learned it in the Low Countries; nor does he appear to have seen any of the superior productions of the Roman, Venetian, and Parisian presses, before he caused his own fount of letters to be cut.

No precise information has been obtained as to the time when Caxton returned to England. In 1477 he had undoubtedly quitted the Continent, and taken up his residence in the neighbourhood of Westminster Abbey, under the patronage of Thomas Milling, Bishop of Hereford and Abbot of Westminster, a man of superior abilities and learning for the times in which he lived. We learn, from a curious placard, a copy of which is still in existence, that Caxton printed in the Almonry.

The commonly-received opinion is that "The Game of Chess" was the first book he printed in England; it was dedicated to George, Duke of Clarence. Caxton enjoyed the royal patronage, and some of the nobility also encouraged him. Whether their favours were of a profitable and substantial nature, does not appear; but (to their honour) it is mentioned that the mercers of London showed themselves great promoters of literature. He was himself indefatigable in cultivating and perfecting this new art, and although, as we have seen, already in the autumn of his days, he laboured with unwearied diligence, and printed, in all, sixty-four works; and, besides the labour necessarily attendant on the superintendence of his press,* he translated most

* "When the impression was finished, Caxton revised a single copy, and corrected the faults with red ink; the copy thus corrected was given to an assistant, to correct the whole impression; and as he was extremely exact, this operation occasioned him much troublesome and minute labour." His printing is inferior in many respects to the printing executed on the Continent during the same period. Mr. Dibdin, however, says that whenever good copies of his books are met with, his type has a bold

of these books into English from the French. In the performance of this task he found no small trouble in his choice of words, for, in those days, the inhabitants ot one county hardly understood those of another; "the common English that is spoken in one shyre varying from another, and certainly," he adds, "the language now used varieth far from that which was used and spoken when I was born." No wonder Caxton was a great deal puzzled and perplexed about the language he should employ in making his translations.

In his selection of works for the press, he was necessarily guided by the public taste, and limited by the difficulty of finding suitable materials, and by the probability of being repaid for his labour and expense. "The Father of Printing," says the historian Gibbon, "expressed a laudable desire to elucidate the history of his country, but, instead of translating the Latin chronicle of Ralph Higden, he could only venture on the English version by John de Trevisa. In the choice of his authors he was reduced to comply with the vicious taste of his readers; to gratify the nobles with treatises of heraldry, hawking, and the game of chess; and to amuse the popular credulity with romances of fabulous knights, and legends of more fabulous saints."

Yet, on the whole—as has been well remarked—

and rich effect, which renders their perusal less painful than that of many foreign productions, where the angular sharpness of the letters somewhat dazzles the eye. All his works were printed in what is called "black letter." Dibdin has givei *fac similes* of his sets or founts of letters. His ink was inferior but his paper fine and good, resembling thin vellum.

when we reflect on the troubled, wasted, and distracted state of the country at that period (he carried on his works during the reigns of Edward V. and Richard III.), we cannot but feel amazed that he did so much, and persisted, amid troubles and confusion, and at such disadvantage, in prosecuting his labours, so as to succeed in establishing the art of printing in his native land.

His last book, "The Lives of the Fathers," he translated from the French, and his admirable assistant and successor, Wynkyn de Worde, says that he finished that work "at the last day of his life."

He died in 1491, and was buried in St. Margaret's Church, Westminster. The date of his birth is generally supposed to have been about 1412.

To him belong the high praise and merit of having, at his own charge and on his sole responsibility, undertaken so great an enterprise, in which, despite all difficulties, he succeeded—thus conferring on his fellow-countrymen an incalculable benefit.

All honour to the "Father of Printing!"

BENVENUTO CELLINI

Born 1500—*Died* 1570.

"Lo! *Welcome** born, I proudly raise my head,—
Fair Florence' son—bright flower of Tuscany."

OF the numerous great and celebrated men who have worked in metal, one of the most renowned is Benvenuto Cellini. The distinguished eminence of this artist in the times of the "old masters," his intimacy with Michael Angelo, Titian, and all the great Italian sculptors and painters of the age, his intercourse with Francis I., Pope Clement VII., the illustrious Duke of Florence, as well as with so many others of the princes, statesmen, and commanders of that turbulent period in which he lived—all these combine to make his history a most remarkable and interesting one. And he has himself given the record of his life, in a very curious piece of autobiography, betokening the genius, eccentricity, and powerful imagination of the man.

He was born in Florence, in 1500, of a family reduced in circumstances, whose ancestors had been territorial lords, trained to the profession of arms. His grandfather, Andrea Cellini, was an architect, and his father, who followed the same calling, was desirous that his son should be brought up to the profession of music; but the lad showed so decided a preference for

* In allusion to his name *Benvenuto*.

the art of design, that it was impossible to keep him from his favourite pursuit; and at fifteen years of age, without his father's consent, he placed himself with a jeweller and goldsmith.

His first essays were made as a chaser and worker in gold; and applying diligently to his business, he soon attained considerable skill, and made so much money that he was able to assist his father and relations, who were poor enough to need his help. He tells us that he "did his utmost to learn the exquisite manner of Michael Angelo Buonarotti, and never once lost sight of it;" and thus describes his first successful performance:—"At this time I produced a piece of basso-relievo in silver, about as big as the hand of a little child; it served for the clasp of a man's belt, clasps of that size being then in use. Upon it was carved a group of foliage, made in the antique taste, with several figures of youths, and other beautiful grotesques. This piece of work I made in the shop of one of my employers; and upon its coming under the inspection of the Goldsmiths' Company, I acquired the reputation of the most expert young man in the trade."

When he was nineteen years old, Benvenuto went to Rome, where he met with great encouragement. His first production was a fine piece of work in silver, to hold a saltcellar, which he adorned with such exquisite figures, that his master made it his boast that his shop had produced such an admirable piece of art. "This was the first money I earned in Rome," he says; "part of it I sent to the relief of my good father, and the remainder I kept to support me while I studied the antiquities of that city." At the end of two years he returned to Florence, where he had every prospect of success in his profession; but his turbulent and irascible temper, which had already involved him in serious difficulty, led him into a quarrel, in which he so severely wounded his adversary, that he was obliged to escape, in the disguise of a friar, to Rome. Here he engaged himself to work at a goldsmith's shop, and was employed by the wife of a wealthy merchant to reset some exceedingly valuable jewellery, for which he received a handsome reward. Afterwards he received a commission from the Bishop of Salamanca to make some chandeliers and silver vases; and before long, chancing to take part in a concert at the Pope's feast, he so much pleased his Holiness, Clement VII., that he took him into his employ in the double capacity of musician and artificer. In the service of this pontiff he executed many of his most beautiful smaller works; and being appointed engraver to the Roman mint, he struck such fine coins and medals as have never been surpassed.

If we should inquire in what way he attained to such perfection in the various branches of his art, we learn, by his own statement, that he with the greatest diligence sought to practise himself first in seal-engraving, afterwards in engraving medals on steel, then in the "most elegant art of enamelling," which he found exceedingly difficult, but took such pleasure in learning that the greatest difficulties appeared to him delightful. Whatever he undertook he pursued with the utmost ardour; and he adds, with great *naïveté*, that all this was "through the peculiar indulgence of the Author of Nature, who had gifted him with so happy a genius that he could with perfect ease learn anything he gave himself to."

As we have said, a very profitable branch of Cellini's labour was that of jewellery. "He set jewels, and adorned them with admirable collets and diminutive figures, so exquisitely formed, and some of them so curious and fanciful, that nothing finer or more beautiful could be conceived." One of his most celebrated productions of this description was a button he made for Pope Clement VII., to be worn upon his pontifical habit, into which he fixed a diamond, with the most exquisite art, having around it figures of children represented on plates of gold, and a central figure admirably engraved.

It would be impossible to give even a slight sketch of the numerous and heart-stirring adventures recorded by this extraordinary man in the history of his life. Europe was at that time involved in the wars between Francis I. and Charles V., in which Italy took an active share. When the Constable Bourbon laid siege to Rome, Cellini took up arms and performed, according to his own account, wonderful acts of valour; and afterwards he distinguished himself in the defence of the Castle of St. Angelo.

In 1534 his great patron, Pope Clement VII. died.

The new pope, Paul III., engaged him in his service; but he had the misfortune to incur the enmity of Pier Luigi, the pontiff's natural son, who persecuted him with relentless animosity. He was accused of having, during the pillage of Rome, stolen the pontifical jewels and other treasures; and although he was able fully to exonerate himself from these charges, he was committed to the Castle of St. Angelo, and treated with the utmost severity. His description of the misery he endured is most fearful; and there seems little doubt that his intellect was affected in consequence of the long confinement he underwent in a dark and damp chamber, where for many months he dragged on a wretched existence. Always addicted to the imaginative, and fond of the marvellous, he ascribed his preservation to supernatural intervention, and believed that he saw a vision which announced his deliverance.

At length his liberation was effected, through the interposition of the French monarch, who was very desirous to secure the services of this great genius Arrived at Fontainebleau, he was received with distinction, and loaded with benefits. The king settled a handsome salary on him, and gave him an order to make several large statues for him in silver.

By the desire of the monarch, he next undertook to ornament the fountains at Fontainebleau, but, failing to pay the necessary court to the Duchess d'Estampes, he incurred her displeasure. His chief offence was, that he had shown the model for one of his statues to the king, without first presenting it for her approval. In consequence, this regal favourite determined to mar the fortune of the uncourteous artist; nor did she rest till he was driven from the kingdom. On one occasion a curious scene occurred. The beautiful statue of Jupiter, having been completed by Cellini, the king was to inspect it on a certain day, but the duchess prevented his going till night. Through her management she had contrived also that some of the finest bronze statues from the antique should be placed in the gallery where the Jupiter was to be shown. "When I saw these wonders of art," said Benvenuto, "I thought within myself, —this is like passing through the pikes of the enemy. Heaven protect me from danger!" He, however, managed, with consummate skill, to light his statue from above, in such a manner, that it was seen to much greater advantage than it could have been under any other circumstances.

The king at length arrived, accompanied by some of the principal nobles and ladies of his court. "When I saw his majesty enter," says the artist, "I ordered my boy, Ascanio, to push the statue of Jupiter before him; and this motion being made with admirable contrivance, caused it to appear alive; so that the other figures were left somewhat behind, and the eyes of all the beholders were first struck with my performance. The king immediately cried out, 'This is one of the finest productions of art that ever was beheld; I, who take pleasure in such things, and understand them, could never have conceived a piece of work the hundredth part so beautiful.'"

This success enraged the favourite, and quickened her desire to be rid of the man who had thus defied her. She was so successful, that Cellini implored, and eventually obtained, the permission of the king to leave the country. Of all his fine works, there now remains in France only the bronze figure of a nymph in bas-relief, to be seen in the museum of the Louvre.

Returning to his native country, our artist entered into the service of the Grand Duke, Cosmo de Medici, who first employed him as a goldsmith, and afterwards in the execution of some fine pieces of sculpture. One of the greatest of these works was the bronze group of Perseus, with the head of Medusa, which was placed in the piazza, near the gate of the ducal palace. This work cost the artist no small labour and difficulty, from various causes. He says, "When it was first seen, the populace set up a loud shout of applause, and there were sonnets in my praise every day upon the gate. At its completion, when it was exposed, just before the break of day, so great a crowd gathered about it, that it is almost impossible to give the reader an idea of their numbers. I behaved as modestly as it was possible for me on the occasion, but the people crowded around me to stare at me more than at my statue." But what crowned the satisfaction of the artist was that those of his own profession emulated each other in commending him; and, indeed, it was surprising that Cellini, having been accustomed to make small figures so many years, should thus happily succeed in bringing so large a work to perfection.

The great Michael Angelo thus wrote to him:—"My dear Benvenuto,—I have many years known you for one of the ablest jewellers in the world, and I now find that you have equal abilities as a sculptor." Shortly after, Cellini, being in Rome, went to visit Michael Angelo, and endeavoured to persuade him to enter the service of the duke at Florence; but he replied that he was now employed in building St. Peter's church, on which account he could not leave Rome. "You have determined on the model of the structure; leave your pupil, Urbino, to work at it in your absence." Finding himself so hardly pressed, the sculptor turned suddenly to his apprentice, as though to ask his opinion on the matter. With rustic gestures and rough voice, the youth exclaimed, "I will never quit Michael Angelo till I have laid him out, or he me." There is something most striking in this anecdote, showing, as it does, how that man of surpassing genius could enchain the affections of his humble assistant.

After the completion of his Perseus, Cellini executed other valuable works, especially a Christ, of life-size, in white marble, on a black crucifix, which has been celebrated as a most exquisite and extraordinary performance.

At the age of sixty, our artist married; and from that time his narrative contains little of general interest. He had several children, and it is evident he was often involved in litigation and embarrassments. On the 16th March, 1563, he had the melancholy honour of being deputed to attend the obsequies of his great master and friend, Michael Angelo Buonarotti. He survived that event seven years, and on the 15th February, 1570, this most extraordinary man and great artist departed this life, and was buried with much pomp in the church of the Annunziata, at Florence.

SIR HUMPHRY DAVY.

Born 1778—*Died* 1829.

"I have neither riches nor birth to recommend me, yet, if I live, I trust I shall not be of less service to mankind and to my friends, than if I had been born with these advantages."

These memorable words were written by Humphry Davy, that illustrious man who had the honour of raising himself to the highest place among the chemical philosophers of his age, emerging from an obscure condition solely by his singular merit. At the time they were penned he was an apothecary's apprentice, to all appearance little likely to make a noise in the world. His father was a carver in wood, at Penzance, in Cornwall, and possessed a small landed property in a village near Penzance, where Davy was born in 1778.

He was early sent to the Grammar School at Truro, kept by a Mr. Coryton, who seems to have been but ill-fitted for his office. He was severe, and punished his pupils for slight offences. One of his favourite inflictions was pulling the boys' ears, and, as Humphry was not disposed to be studious overmuch, he frequently suffered from this propensity, till, in order to save himself, he had recourse to an ingenious artifice. One day he made his appearance before the master with a large plaister on each ear, and being asked what ailed his ears, he replied, with a very grave face, that he had put on the plaisters to prevent a mortification!

Writing, in after years, to his mother, he said, "I consider it fortunate that I was left much to myself as a child, and put upon no particular plan of study, and that I enjoyed much idleness at Mr. Coryton's school. I perhaps owe to these circumstances the little talents that I have, and their peculiar application. What I am, I have made myself. I say this without vanity, and in pure simplicity of heart."

Out of school he was very popular; one great cause of which was his powers of diverting his comrades by telling them stories—commonly of wonder and terror, which were so attractive that he was sure to have a numerous audience. His brother relates, that the earliest indication he gave of his fondness for experimenting was in making fireworks, his eldest sister being his assistant in compounding the ingredients of the squibs and crackers. To one of his compositions he gave the name of "thunder powder," which he used to explode on a stone, to the great delight of his playfellows.

When he was sixteen years of age he lost his father, who left a young widow with five children, of whom Humphry was the eldest. This event seemed to have had a powerful effect on him; he relinquished all his boyish habits, and, with steady resolution, set himself to work. Seeing his mother one day in great affliction, he, in a most affectionate manner, begged her not to grieve, saying that "he would do all he could for his brother and sisters." And faithfully did he redeem his promise.

To his mother he appears to have been fondly attached, and, indeed, she was a woman of excellent qualities, placid in temper, kind and benevolent, of sound understanding, and perfect integrity. His boyish home had been a happy one, though humble.

He was now apprenticed to an apothecary at Penzance, but, disliking the business, he occupied himself with chemical experiments, ingeniously contriving to make the utensils of the shop and the kitchen serve for apparatus; and not unfrequently he alarmed the household by his explosions. No wonder the apothecary voted him "a troublesome fellow," of whom he was glad to be rid. Endowed with an original, independent, and somewhat eccentric mind, the apprentice had studied after a fashion of his own, to good purpose. His note-books, written during that time, showed the ardour with which he entered on his pursuits, and the various branches of knowledge he proposed to follow. One of them, bearing date 1795, contained a plan of study, with essays, metaphysical, moral, and religious. Curiously enough, outside one of the covers there was the figure of an ancient lyre, drawn by his pen, and on the other an olive-leaf, encircling a lamp. Could it be that, already, at the age of 17, he had formed a latent idea of his great discovery?

It happened fortunately, at this time, that Mr. G. Watt, son of the great engineer, came to reside in the house of Davy's mother at Penzance, being ordered to pass the winter there for his health. The conversation and advice of one so skilled in science and letters, was a great advantage to the embryo philosopher, of which he gladly availed himself. Another accident brought him acquainted with Mr. Davies Gilbert, by whom he was assisted in various ways, and introduced to Dr. Beddoes, who had then recently opened a Pneumatic Institution at Bristol, for the medical uses of gases, and for investigating their properties. The result was the appointment of young Davy to the post of superintendent of this institution; and thus he found himself at once enabled to pursue his scientific vocation as a profession.

It was not long before the young philosopher published the result of various curious experiments he had made in medical and physical science, which gained him considerable repute as an experimental chemist; and in 1802 he was chosen Chemical Professor, by the Royal Institution of London.

"He had now invaluable helps to his pursuits, an ample command of books, assistants under him, above all, an unlimited power of collecting and making apparatus. His income was secure, and his time was at his own disposal." Nor did he fail diligently to avail himself of these great advantages. During the five following years he continued his experiments, and at the end of that time communicated to the Royal Society some discoveries relative to the laws of electrical and chemical action, which excited the deepest interest in the philosophical world.

"It thus appeared certain," says Lord Brougham, "that an indissoluble connection exists between chemical and electric action, if, indeed, it was not even proved that chemical affinity and electricity are identical. The science of electro-chemistry, at all events, now arose out of Davy's discoveries, and he is entitled to be regarded as its founder. It may easily be conceived that these important truths excited generally the anxious attention of philosophers. The French National Institute, greatly to their honour, though the war between the two countries never raged more fiercely than now, crowned Davy with the first honour founded by Napoleon for scientific desert."

At this time he was twenty-eight years old; and his appearance is thus described by Lady Brownrigg in writing to Dr. John Davy:—"We had been invited by Dr. Richardson to go to his cottage at Portrush, to meet the famous Mr. Davy. We arrived a short time before dinner, and in passing through a room saw a youth—as he appeared—who had come in from fishing, and who, with a little note-book, was seated in a window-seat, having left bag, rod, &c., on the ground. He was very intent on this little book, and we passed unnoticed. When I went into the drawing-room I felt some little awe at this great philosopher, annexing to such a character at least the idea of an elderly grave gentleman; certainly, I never calculated on being introduced to the identical youth, with a little brown head like a boy, at the window-seat, and who, when I came into the drawing-room was in the most animated manner recounting an adventure which had entertained him on the causeway; and from his mode of telling it was causing loud laughing in the whole room. The evening passed very agreeably. After supper a most interesting occurrence took place. A gentleman of the company, when the ladies had retired, thought proper to commence an attack upon revealed religion, and avowed himself a professed sceptic. There were two clergymen present, whom he hoped to silence by gaining over to his side the great philosopher; and he continued for some time to utter his infidel opinions, encouraged by the silent and deep attention with which Davy listened to him. At length he paused, full of triumphant expectation, when, to the delight of some of the company, the man of genius, with deep earnestness, and in eloquent language, defended the truth of Christianity. So striking and impressive was his manner, that one of the clergymen (the Bishop of Raphoe) *stood up* from an involuntary impulse, like that which has sometimes called a whole audience to their feet at some burst of religious fervour from an eloquent preacher. The discomfited infidel retired in dismay, nor did he venture again to show his face in that company."

This illustrious chemist having thus arrived at the laws of electrical action, applied his great principle to the analyses of the vegetable alkalies, and in the following year discovered the two metals to which he gave the names of *potassium* and *sodium*. "The glory of having now made the greatest discovery of the age was plainly Davy's," continues Lord Brougham, "and it was not the result of happy accident, but of laborious investigation, conducted with a skill and a patience equally admirable, and according to the strict rules of the soundest philosophy."*

But the most valuable discovery which this great man offered to humanity was his Safety Lamp. Had he invented nothing else, he would deservedly enjoy the lasting gratitude of all true friends of man. The terrible ravages made on human life by the fire-damp explosions—that is, the burning of hydrogen gas in mines—had often attracted the attention of the mine-owner and the philanthropist. In his boyhood Davy had doubtless often listened to disastrous tales of these fearful accidents. In 1812 a most terrible explosion occurred in a colliery near Sunderland, accompanied by an awful sacrifice of life. This catastrophe led to the formation of the Society for the Prevention of Accidents in Coal-mines; and it was at the request of the members of that body that the attention of Davy was directed to the subject. After fully ascertaining the cause of the fire-damp, he made a series of experiments, which resulted in the discovery that "gauze of wire, whose meshes were only one twenty-

* The delight which he experienced when he first saw the minute globules of potassium (the new metal) burst through the crust of potash, and take fire as they entered the atmosphere, was witnessed by his relative (Mr. E. Davy), who says:—"He actually danced about the room with ecstatic delight, and some little time was required for him to compose himself sufficiently to continue the experiment."

second of an inch diameter, stopped the flame, and prevented the explosion. The candle or lamp being wrapped in such gauze, and all access to the external air prevented, except through the meshes, the lamp may be safely introduced into a gallery filled with fire-damp; a feeble blue flame will take place inside the gauze, but no explosion, even if the wire be heated nearly red."

One of his friends, who had assisted him in his experiments, says: "Sir H. Davy accompanied me into some of our fiery mines, to prove the efficacy of his lamp. Nothing could be more gratifying than the result of the trial, as it inspired everybody with perfect confidence in the security which his invention had afforded. He was himself delighted, and I was overpowered with feelings of gratitude to the great genius who had produced it."

This lamp, more marvellous than the magical one of Aladdin, has saved the lives of thousands of miners. The illustrious inventor generously gave to the public the whole benefit of the invention, and thus sacrificed the rich profit which he might have secured to himself by a patent. "My sole object," said he, "was to serve the cause of humanity; and I am amply rewarded by the reflection that I have been enabled to do so." *

* The value of this great invention was everywhere recognized. The Royal Society honoured it with their medals; some of the great proprietors of the collieries voted to Sir Humphry Davy a splendid service of silver plate, of the value of £1,200; and the Emperor Alexander of Russia presented him with a beautiful silver-gilt vase, accompanied by a letter from himself expressing his admiration of the important discovery.

So early as 1806 he had been chosen a foreign associate of the French Institute. In 1816 he was created a baronet; and on the death of Sir Joseph Banks, in 1820, Sir Humphry Davy was unanimously chosen to succeed him as President of the Royal Society, and continued to fill that distinguished office until, his health having failed, he resigned it in 1827. Already he had suffered from a serious illness in 1807, in consequence of the prolonged labour and excitement attending his grand discoveries, and was for many months incapable of carrying on his work. During that sickness, his heart turned with fond longing to the home of his boyhood. "No Swiss peasant," says one of his biographers, "ever sighed more deeply for his native mountains than did he for the scenes of his early years. He entreated his nurse to convey to his friends his ardent wish to have some apples from a particular tree which he had planted when a boy; and he remained in a state of restlessness and impatience till their arrival." There is something very touching in this little incident. It adds one more to the numerous examples which show that whatever our destiny, and however fortune may have changed our condition, the deep affections of our nature cling fondly to the simplicities of our childhood, and the heart is cheered and warmed by the remembrance of early joys.

This illustrious man was not spoiled by the marvellous success which crowned his efforts, nor did the flattery of an applauding world render him deaf to the fond pleas of dutiful love. No sooner was he in a situation that secured him the necessaries of life, than he remembered his mother and sisters, and generously supplied his brother with the means of prosecuting his studies. To one and another of "*the old pensioners*," that knew him in early life, he sent tokens of remembrance, and bade his sisters "buy some ribbons or little articles of dress" for the maid-servants of the family and some friends. Nor can we omit to mention that he left at his death a paper of directions, in which he desired that the interest from £100 stock might be annually paid to the master of the Penzance Grammar-school, on condition that the boys should *have a holiday on his birthday.* Surely this simple trait reveals the workings of an affectionate heart. The great philosopher was a man to be loved as much as admired.

A singular proof of the admiration in which his name was held by his countrymen, and how well it became known, even among the common people, is thus related :—"Returning home one evening, he observed an ordinary man showing the moon and a planet through a telescope placed upon the pavement. He went up and paid his pence for a look ; but no such thing would they permit. 'That's Sir Humphry Davy,' ran among the people ; and the exhibitor, returning the money, said, with an important air, which exceedingly delighted him, 'that he could not think of taking anything from a brother philosopher.'"

The principal relaxations in which Sir H. Davy

had indulged during the intervals of his laborious exertions were shooting, and especially fishing, of which he was, from his earliest years, passionately fond. When, at the end of 1826, he returned from his foreign tour, he published a book called "Salmonia," on this favourite pursuit. His latest work—"The last Days of a Philosopher"—was written in the following year, when he again went to the Continent, in search of health. He passed the winter at Rome, and in the spring of 1829 travelled to Geneva, where, on the 29th May, he expired suddenly of an apoplectic attack. He had barely attained his fifty-first year.

SEBASTIAN ERARD & CLAUDE MONTAL.

PIANOFORTE-MAKING AND TUNING.

ERARD, *born* 1752—*died* 1831.

How much are the lovers of chamber music indebted to those skilful mechanics whose talent has been devoted to the invention and perfection of the harp and the pianoforte. In former times the spinet and harpsichord, with their harsh and discordant sounds, were much in vogue; they are now happily consigned to oblivion, and have been succeeded by that fine musical instrument the piano, originally invented by a Florentine in the service of the Duke of Tuscany. The first instruments of this kind were very imperfect in touch and mechanism, and but slow progress was made in their improvement for a considerable period.

One of the celebrated names in this department of mechanical science and skill is *Sebastian Erard*, whose pianos deservedly attained such great repute both in this country and in France. He was born in Strasburg in 1752, and was the fourth child of a cabinet maker of that city. When a mere lad he showed a bold and aspiring disposition,—one of his feats being to mount to the summit of Strasburg cathedral, and perch himself upon its cross.* It was first intended that he

* The tower of this celebrated cathedral, one of the finest

should be brought up as an architect; and from the age of eight years he studied perspective and linear drawing, to which he added a course of practical geometry. This first education proved very useful to him in his after-career, and facilitated the discoveries which afterwards rendered him celebrated. He acquired, above all, a great aptitude in expressing his ideas by drawing, which spared him a good deal of useless expense.

His father having died, the young man was left to pursue his own course, and at the age of eighteen he went to Paris and apprenticed himself to a harpsichord-maker, in whose service he soon became a skilful workman. His great talent was quickly displayed in an extraordinary degree, so much so as to excite the jealousy of his employer.

He had not long come out of his apprenticeship before he was employed by another maker, who, aware of his skill in invention, proposed to Erard to execute an instrument of a novel description, differing from the common harpsichord; by a private engagement, however, it was settled that the name of the employer should appear upon it. When it was completed, the amateur who purchased it, delighted with its excellence, returned to make inquiries of the harpsichord-maker as to the nature of the improvements, and asked him a host of questions about the internal mechanism, which the man, taken by surprise, was wholly unable to

specimens of Gothic architecture in existence, is 470 feet high, and is said to be the loftiest building in the world, with the exception of the highest of the pyramids of Egypt.

answer; at length, he was forced to confess that it was the work of young Erard.

Of this invention, which he called the *clavecin méchanique*, a detailed account appeared in the Musical Almanac of 1776. It was pronounced a *chef-d'œuvre* of invention and execution, and at once made the reputation of the young artisan.

The Duchess de Villeroi, a great patroness of the arts, took him under her protection, and it was in the Hôtel de Villeroi that his first piano was constructed. This instrument was then almost unknown in France, and had only recently been introduced in Germany. The duchess was desirous to have one, and she wished that, if possible, it should be made by a Frenchman: at her instigation, Erard determined to try his powers; and after having examined one of German construction, belonging to the inhabitants of a neighbouring house, he commenced the task, which he accomplished in a short time; and a scientific comparison being made between the two instruments, Erard's was pronounced superior.

Listened to in Madame de Villeroi's saloons, in which the most distinguished musical amateurs and professors were accustomed to assemble, it made a great sensation, and the fortune of the skilful artist was secured.

He soon established himself in business, and was joined by his brother John Baptiste. At first they encountered much opposition from the jealousy and ill-will of some of the manufacturers, but success in the end crowned their meritorious efforts, and the sale of their pianofortes steadily increased. These instruments found their way throughout France, the Netherlands, and some parts of Germany; and in the year 1799 a commission in Hamburg sold one hundred of Erard's pianos.

Among the numerous improvements introduced by this maker, was that of adapting the instrument to voices of moderate power. For this purpose he conceived the idea of rendering the key of the piano moveable in either direction to the extent of half a note, a whole note, or a note and a half. This ingenious contrivance was first tried in a piano which he made for the queen, Marie Antoinette, whose voice was of small compass. It was also on this instrument he made the first trial of the *orgue expressif*, in which, by the prolonged pressure of a finger, the sound was diminished or increased at pleasure, like the inflexions of the voice. The harp was at that time a very fashionable instrument, and Erard's attention was consequently directed toward it, with the design to obviate some of the great inconveniences of its construction, as it was then made. His projects were interrupted by the outbreak of the French revolution in 1789, and he hastened to quit France for England, where he remained several years. He formed a flourishing establishment in London, his reputation there being very considerable, and the sale of his instruments proportionably large.

Returning to Paris in 1796, he produced his improved grand pianoforte, which increased his scientific repute, and completed the numerous improvements and additions he had introduced into pianoforte-making. Returning to England, Erard, in 1811, crowned his successes by the beautiful and difficult invention of the harp with two pedals. Its success was immense: not only was the form of the instrument improved, giving it more elegance, but the richness of the sound was tripled by means of pedals and levers, skilfully combined to correspond to the same sounds of the octave on different strings. In 1815, Erard, being at Paris, presented it for examination at the Institute, when M. de Prony, in the name of the Academy of Sciences and of the Fine Arts united, made a highly-flattering report on its merits.

So many important contributions to the advancement of his art had deservedly procured for M. Erard the suffrages of learned men, artists and amateurs. He had received the gold medal at every examination of the products of French industry, and was the first musical-instrument-maker who obtained the cross of the Legion of Honour; rewards deservedly conferred on one whose life had been spent in unremitting labour for the advancement of an art which imparts so great a charm to the domestic and social circle. Happily, the personal character of M. Erard was such as to command respect and esteem. "He possessed," says M. Foucaud, "the rare quality of making himself beloved by all those employed in his service, sharing their labours, and rejoicing in their improvement. He always spoke to them in tones of encouragement, and assisted them when in difficulties, not only by advice, but with his purse, which was always open to them. He gave pensions to aged mechanics, or such as were in extreme poverty, and carried his generosity to such a degree, that he would aid those of his own trade in founding establishments on as large a scale as his own.

" Apprentices are considered an ungrateful class, but good masters make good workmen ; and if such a man as Erard were at the head of every manufactory, we should probably hear fewer of these complaints."

This worthy man suffered, during the closing years of his life, from a most painful malady. His last work was the grand organ which he built for the chapel of the Tuileries—an admirable production, worthy the reputation of its maker.

On occasion of his death, which took place in August, 1831, his workmen paid a pleasing tribute to his memory. They raised a subscription among themselves, with the proceeds of which a bust of Erard was executed ; and the day devoted to the inauguration of this monument of their affection and regret was one which deeply affected them.

Since the time of Sebastian Erard, great improvements have been made in the pianoforte, and the English manufacturers especially maintained for a long time a marked superiority in this branch of the trade. We cannot refrain, in connection with this subject, from mentioning an individual whose remarkable efforts excite both astonishment and admiration, and who affords a new and striking example of the "pursuit of knowledge under difficulties." To M. Foucaud we are indebted for the following account of *Claude Montal*, who, blind from a very early age, owes to his own energy and talent the high reputation he has gained in the musical world. Some years ago, he filled, with great credit to himself, the office of tutor in the Institution for the Blind, founded by M. Hauy. Here it was that he passed his childhood and youth, and expected to spend his future life in instructing his companions in affliction.

An accidental circumstance excited his attention to an entirely different and new mode of gaining his subsistence. He heard that much money might be earned by tuning pianos; and the idea took possession of his mind. After thinking much upon the subject, he resolved to study the mechanism of those instruments. With his small savings he purchased a piano, and, little by little, gained a perfect acquaintance with all its parts, till he was completely master of the details of its construction.

He paid some young men to read such works to him as might assist him in his researches, and in this manner he soon attained great skill in tuning pianos. By degrees the fame of his talent spread; the most celebrated professors took a pleasure in encouraging him, and before long he was esteemed to rank at the head of his art. He became, in fact, the only *professor of tuning* in France; and, still further, he published a valuable treatise on the theory of his art, entitled, *The Art of Tuning one's own Piano.* His next step was to become himself a piano-maker, in which he succeeded so completely as to be honoured with the approbation of connoisseurs, and to attain an honourable place among his compeers.

Such remarkable efforts must appear truly astonishing, when we consider the difficulties with which this remarkable man has had to struggle. Blind, without fortune or master, he has acquired a distinguished rank in his art—one which requires long and persevering study.

GRAHAM AND BREGUET.

CLOCK AND WATCH MAKING.

GRAHAM, *born* 1675—*died* 1751. BREGUET, *born* 1747—*died* 1823.

> "My watch, the solitary kind companion
> Of my imprisonment—my faithful watch
> Hangs by."

THE science of mechanics applied to watchmaking, reveals a world of wonders; and hosts of ingenious artisans have distinguished themselves in the different branches of nautical, astronomical, and domestic horology. It would be impossible to mention the names alone of those who excelled in these various departments. We are compelled to confine ourselves to two only of the most illustrious. One, a countryman of our own, named *George Graham*, was, without competition, the most eminent of his profession at the time when he lived, not only in the particular department of his calling as a clock and watch maker, but as a general mechanician. This admirable man was born of Quaker parentage at Horsgills, in the county of Cumberland, in the year 1675, and when only thirteen years old was apprenticed to a watchmaker in London. His intelligence and good conduct were so satisfactory that, after he had remained some time with his master, he was taken, purely on account of his good conduct, into the family of the celebrated Mr. Tompion, an English watchmaker of deserved renown. This gentleman perceiving in his young *protégé* indications of remarkable talent, united with great excellence of character and high principle, became much interested in his progress, and treated him with an almost parental affection throughout his life. It was not long before his abilities were strikingly displayed; gifted with inventive sagacity, he, at the same time, took the most scrupulous care in the execution of his work. In process of time he became not only a first-rate watchmaker, but the best general mechanic of his day. He also obtained a complete knowledge of practical astronomy, and was thus enabled to give to various movements for measuring time a degree of perfection which had never before been attained; and also invented several astronomical instruments by which the science was greatly advanced. We are told that by a wonderful manual dexterity "he was enabled to construct them with greater precision and accuracy than any other person in the world." That this high praise was not unmerited will be perceived by a glance at what he effected. Among other valuable works of his was a grand mural arch in the observatory at Greenwich, made for Dr. Halley, under Mr. Graham's immediate inspection, and divided by his own hand; from this incomparable original the best foreign instruments have been copied. It was by the aid of a sector of his invention, that Dr. Bradley first discovered two new motions in the fixed stars. By his skill he comprised the whole planetary system within the compass of a small cabinet, which invention served as a model for the orreries of the eighteenth century; and when the French academicians were projecting their voyage to the north pole, for the purpose of ascertaining the figure of the earth, Mr. Graham was judged to be the fittest person in Europe to supply them with instruments. How well he justified the choice was seen, when, aided by his works, those operations were completed in one year; whereas, those members of the expedition who went to the south, not being so well furnished, were greatly embarrassed and retarded in their progress. For several years this distinguished man was a member of the Royal Society of London, to which he imparted several ingenious and important discoveries, chiefly on astronomical and philosophical subjects; and he continued to make experiments in his favourite sciences till almost the period of his death, which took place at his house in Fleet Street, Nov. 20, 1751, in his 76th year. He was buried in Westminster Abbey, in the same grave with his friend and predecessor—the celebrated Tompion. Of his personal character the most pleasing accounts have been preserved. He seems to have delighted in acts of generosity, and to have had for his main object the advancement of science, and the benefit of his fellow-men. Actuated by the strictest integrity, he was above suspicion, and his liberality in communicating to others the results of his experiments won him th esteem of his compeers. It is said he frequently lent money, but he could never be prevailed on to take any interest; nor did he ever place out any money on Government securities He had bank-notes which were thirty years old in his possession at the time of his death; and his whole property, with the exception of his stock in trade, was found in a strong box. Had he been an avaricious man, the contents of that treasury would have been a hundredfold greater; but he had saved enough to supply his wants, and to enable him to relieve the necessities of others. There is a characteristic story of him which shows what a degree of exactness he attained in his workmanship, and how high was his estimate of it.

A person who had ordered a watch of him, when he took it out of his hands, said that he was going abroad, to reside nearly five years in India, and that he wished to know to what point he might reckon upon the regularity of its movements. "Friend," replied the worthy Quaker, "it is a watch I have made and regulated myself; carry it where thou wilt; if, at the end of five years thou come back to me, and canst say it has varied five minutes, I will return thy money." The purchaser, after an absence of rather more than five years, made his appearance at the watchmaker's, and, affecting a serious manner, said,—"I bring you back your watch, sir." "I remember my promise," said Graham; "show me the watch." "Well (after examining it), what dost thou complain of?" "What do I complain of? why, that it has varied more than five minutes during the five years I have had it." "In that case I return thy money," said the other, suiting the action to the words. "What do you mean?" "I mean that I fulfil my engagement" (pocketing the watch). "I would not give up the watch, Mr. Graham, for ten times the amount I paid you for it." "And I, on my part, will on no account withdraw from my engagement. A promise with me is a sacred thing. I promised thee, on certain conditions, to receive back the watch; in consequence of that promise, thou hast returned it to me, and no power on earth shall compel me to relinquish my treaty." He kept his word; and to the day of his death, that watch served him as a regulator. It is said, he was fond of entertaining his customers with this anecdote, though usually not disposed to be facetious.

That Graham's watches were held in the highest estimation by the noble as well as the scientific, appears from the following anecdote:—The French mathematician Maupertius, who did much to encourage horology, and was considered an admirable judge of the art, was made prisoner at the battle of Molnitz, and taken to Vienna. The grand-duke of Tuscany, afterwards emperor, delighted at seeing a man of such great reputation, treated him with much kindness, and asked whether there were any particular part of his property which the hussars had taken from him that he especially valued.

Being much pressed, the philosopher acknowledged

that he wished to have saved a watch of Graham's, of which he made use in his astronomical observations. The duke had also one by the same maker, but adorned with diamonds. "So," said he, taking it from his pocket, "it was but a joke; they have brought it to me, and I now return it."

This eminent man's mercurial pendulum is still used in the best regulators, his dead escapement is generally used in astronomical timekeepers, while his horizontal or cylinder escapement is used, with few exceptions, in all the best watches made in France and Switzerland.

As has been said, he was buried in the nave of Westminster Abbey, in the same grave with his friend and master, Thomas Tompion. The slab bore the following inscription:—"Here lies the body of Thos. Tompion, who died Nov. 20, 1713, aged 75. Also Geo. Graham, watchmaker, and F.R.S., whose curious inventions do honour to the British genius, whose accurate performances are the standard of mechanic skill. He died the 16th November, 1751, in the 78th year of his age."

Watchmakers, we are assured,* were (until prevented by recent restrictions) in the habit of making frequent pilgrimages to this spot, feeling, as they gazed upon this tribute, proud of their occupation, while many a secret wish to excel arose as they contemplated the resting-place of two men they so much

* See a little vol. entitled "Time and Timekeepers," by Adam Thompson.

revered. Their memory may last, but the slab, alas! is gone, having been removed by the authorities in 1838, and in its place there remains only a small lozenge-shaped bit of marble bearing their names and the dates of their death.

The name of Bréguet has attained a European renown; and the particulars of his history are full of interest. He was born at Neufchatel, in Switzerland, in 1747, of one of the numerous French families driven into exile by the revocation of the Edict of Nantes. His family were in reduced circumstances, and his father having died when he was still a child, his mother married a clockmaker, who endeavoured to teach the boy his trade. At school he had appeared hopelessly stupid, and his master pronounced him deficient in intellect. Nor did he at first show any inclination to take to the sedentary occupation of his father-in-law. But by degrees he became interested in mechanical experiments; and his intelligence, being thus called into play, was not long in developing itself It was soon joined to a studious perseverance, certain in the end to reap its deserved reward.

When he was fifteen years old he was taken by his parents to Paris, and placed with a watchmaker at Versailles. The time of his apprenticeship being expired, and his master expressing the satisfaction his industry and good conduct had given him, the lad made him the following reply:—

"I have a favour, sir, to ask of you. I am conscious that I have not employed all my time to the best of my ability while in your service; and I wish to be allowed to work three months longer under you, without salary."

This request originated a friendship between the master and his conscientious apprentice, who a short time after found himself, by the death of both his parents, left an orphan, and charged with the support of his little sister. His resolution and industry triumphed over all difficulties; and feeling an ardent desire to complete his education, he determined to acquire a knowledge of mathematics, perceiving that this was indispensable to the perfection of his art. By working over-hours, the high-spirited youth found time to listen to a course of lectures on this subject, delivered by the Abbé Marie, who, observing his punctual attendance and earnest looks, noticed and befriended him.

From that period the course of the young artist was a progressive one. In surmounting the difficulties of his position, his ideas had advanced, and he had gained skill in his art, and soon his works acquired a name. It chanced one day that the duke of Orleans, being in London, showed a watch of Bréguet's to the celebrated watchmaker Arnold, who, at that time, was reckoned the first of his art in Europe.* The beautiful machinery, and the completeness of the parts in this

* Arnold introduced several improvements in the mechanism of timekeepers, and was the inventor of the expansion-balance, &c. Before him the celebrated John Harrison had invented his famous chronometer for taking the longitude at sea, which gained Queen Anne's premium of £20,000.

work, filled him with admiration, and so much was he delighted that, eager to make acquaintance with Bréguet, he immediately set off for Paris. The result was a strong mutual regard between the two men, which was so great that the English watchmaker left his son for two years with Bréguet, in order that he might be instructed by so great a master in the principles of their art. This is a truly pleasing and instructive example of mutual confidence and good will, worthy of the imitation of men of genuine talent, who are too often kept apart by a spirit of jealous rivalry. Before the revolution broke out in France, Bréguet had already founded the establishment which afterwards produced so many masterpieces of mechanism and clockmaking, and his reputation was rapidly increasing. Although quite indifferent to politics, he fell under the suspicion of the dominant party, and owed his safety only to the interposition of some friends, at whose solicitation he was permitted to leave France. He repaired to England, where he lived two years, and, by the generous assistance of a kind friend, was enabled to continue, without embarrassment, his mechanical researches, together with his son, who had accompanied him in his exile.

On his return to France, he found his establishment had been destroyed, but he opened a new one, and eventually it became more prosperous and successful than the former.

M. Bréguet died in 1823, leaving behind him a personal character not less remarkable than his professional talent. So great were the attractions of his manners and conversation that the best society of Paris welcomed him to their circles, and among them he found some of his most intimate friends. It is said that he retained the *naïveté* of youth and even of childhood, and found something to admire everywhere, save in his own productions. He was simple, consistent, and equable in temper. Timid, without losing self-possession; and, in some respects, he was thought to resemble the excellent La Fontaine. Modest and retiring, he would never quit the humble abode in which fortune had crowned his industry and skill: there he delighted to welcome the promising young men of his own trade, to whom he was always a firm friend, and many of whom he was able to assist, from the deep interest he took in their welfare. He made all around him happy, and was himself the happiest of the whole. Even the infirmities of increasing age did not diminish his zest for social intercourse; and when death overtook him, he was busily engaged in a work upon horology.

For a just appreciation of Bréguet's labours, we cannot do better than refer to the statement of the judicious critic M. Charles Dupin. He tells us that this celebrated clockmaker brought all parts of his art to such perfection that nothing can be more delicate and ingenious than his mechanism. He particularizes his detached escapement and also that called *natural*, where no oil is required, and in the mechanism of which there is no spring. Another, and still finer work, is that of the duplex escapement. Bréguet also contrived a plan for preserving the mechanism of portable marine watches or chronometers from the injury caused by the rolling and pitching of vessels, and, still further, discovered a method to prevent their movements being deranged even by a blow or a fall to the ground.

An English officer, General Brisbane, had one of these chronometers, which he subjected to the greatest trials, by constantly wearing it on horseback, and during several long voyages. In sixteen months, its greatest variation was only a second and a half.

At the time when Bréguet accomplished this admirable result, the English Parliament had offered a reward of 250,000 francs* to the artist who would make a chronometer for ships which should not exceed two seconds. No one had gained this prize when he exceeded the limit as above stated.

The renown of Bréguet's name has been maintained by the skill of his nephew, who carries on his uncle's studies with great success, and retains the gold medal in the family.

* Upwards of £10,000.

LORENZO GHIBERTI & QUINTIN MATSYS.

GHIBERTI, *b.* 1380—*d.* 1456. MATSYS, *b.* 1466—*d.* 1529.

THE art of working in metal has ever been highly esteemed, and many artisans of the middle ages have left masterpieces of beauty in this department, testifying the taste and industry with which they wrought; but the annals of those times are very sparing of the names of the men whose works now excite the admiration of connoisseurs, as they gaze on models of finish both in design and execution.

At the end of the thirteenth century, a goldsmith named Raoul, renowned for his talents in this line, was ennobled under the reign of Philip the Bold. This was the first instance of honourable distinction conferred on one belonging to the working classes in France.

At a somewhat later period flourished the two distinguished artists *Lorenzo Ghiberti* and *Quintin Matsys.* The first of these will ever be remembered by his celebrated work, the bronze gates of the Baptistery of Florence, of which copies in miniature, executed by M. Barbidienne of Paris, were shown at the great exhibition of 1851.

Ghiberti was born in Florence, towards the close of the fourteenth century. He received his first instructions from his stepfather, who practised the art of the goldsmith, at that time much in repute (especially with the Florentines), and which extended to the designing of all kinds of ornamental work in metals. The youth learned drawing, the art of modelling and casting metals, and he also acquired some knowledge of painting; so that, when obliged, in consequence of a pestilence which desolated his native city, and the distressed state of affairs consequent thereupon, to fly thence to Rimini, he found employment in painting a fresco in one of the princely palaces there.

He tells us how, with great diligence and ardour, he applied to his task, his mind being quite turned toward the study of painting; but, scarcely had he completed his fresco, when a circumstance occurred which afforded him the opportunity of signalizing himself, not only as the greatest artist of his own time, but as one whose works have commanded the admiration of after-ages. This was the competition for a second pair of brazen doors for the Baptistery at Florence, worthy to accompany those of Andrea Pisano. executed about 1340. This memorable competition attracted all the artists of the highest eminence, and from among them seven were selected to make trial of their skill, including Donatello, Brunelleschi, and Ghiberti. The first of these, a youthful artist, scarcely eighteen years of age, had already attracted public notice. A year was given them to produce a model in bas-relief for one of the panels—the subject being the sacrifice of Isaac. At the end of that time, thirty-four of the most skilful sculptors, painters and goldsmiths of the day were chosen as umpires, and the judgment was to be pronounced in public, in presence of a large assembly gathered together for the occasion.

There is something very interesting in the account of what transpired. The works of the three artists whom we have named were immediately selected as superior to the rest. It remained to decide between these. While judgment was still in suspense, Brunelleschi and Donatello retired together apart, and, confessing to each other that Ghiberti's work was superior to theirs, they magnanimously came forward, and publicly announced their conviction that such was the case. This opinion was confirmed by the umpires, amid the general applause of the assembly.

The victorious competitor was desired to spare neither time nor expense to produce a work worthy of himself and of the republic, and the result was the execution of those beautiful gates which the great Michael Angelo pronounced, in an ecstasy of delight, worthy to be the gates of Paradise! The first, on which Ghiberti was engaged for twenty-one years, is divided into twenty panels, adorned with bas-reliefs, representing various subjects from the New Testament. He afterwards executed for the same building another pair of bronze doors, containing ten reliefs, on a larger scale, from Old Testament subjects. This work, which far exceeded the other in perfection of design, occupied the artist almost as long a time.

Among various other beautiful works by Ghiberti

were his bronze statues of St. John the Baptist, St. Matthew, and St. Stephen, for the church of St. Michael in Florence, and an admirable bronze relief in the Duomo at Florence, representing a saint raising a dead child to life.

This great artist exerted a vast influence on the progress of taste, and from him dates a new epoch in the history of Italian and modern art generally. He was consulted by artists and their patrons about all important undertakings, and the pupils formed under his instructions were many of them celebrated as the leading designers and artists of their time.

The exact period of his death is unknown; but it is supposed to have happened shortly after he made his will, which was dated November, 1455, when he was about seventy-seven years old.

QUINTIN MATSYS, known under the name of "The Blacksmith of Antwerp," received that title from the fact that, during his earlier years, he followed that trade, or rather that of a locksmith. He was born in 1466, and his history is a pathetic one. When very young he lost his father, and was left, with no other dependence for his own subsistence, and that of his mother, but his toil. In addition to poverty, he had to struggle with feeble health, and in his twentieth year a dreadful sickness brought him to the point of death. By this affliction he was greatly reduced, and not feeling equal to the more laborious parts of his business, he turned his attention to the decorative style, in which he soon gave evidence of great ability.

He first undertook to cover and surround, with a net of iron work, a well near the great church of Antwerp. This work was remarkable for the delicacy of the execution, and the good taste of the ornaments with which it was decorated. Shortly after, he made, for the College of Louvain, an iron balustrade, equally admirable in design. But even this kind of work was too laborious for his strength, and again his health threatened to give way. A friend of Matsys, who knew his taste in drawing, now advised him to attempt a different description of work. It was then the custom, on occasion of the solemn annual processions of the Roman Catholic Church, to distribute among the people small images of saints, which were executed for this purpose. Much skill and taste were employed in the production of such works, and Matsys soon excelled in them.

We have seen Ghiberti, at one period of his life, on the point of relinquishing that branch of art in which he afterwards obtained such renown, for the painter's easel, and well it was that chance turned him from his purpose.

A romantic incident induced Matsys to lay aside his first calling, and to become a painter. He fell in love, and the object of his attachment was the fair daughter of a painter of Antwerp, who designed her for one of his pupils. It appears that his mistress returned his affection, but there was an insuperable barrier opposed to the accomplishment of their happiness. The damsel would by no means demean herself to marry a blacksmith; she was determined to have a painter for her husband, and if he wished for her hand, he must outpaint the suitor whom her father favoured!

Thus, incited by love and ambition combined, Quentin shut himself up, and studied the art of painting with the utmost diligence. At length, thinking himself a match for his rival, he carried one of his performances to her father, who, surprised and delighted with the production, consented to receive him for a son-in-law. On the tomb which was erected to Matsys 100 years after his death in the cathedral of Antwerp, there is engraven in letters of gold, this line:—

"*Connubialis amor de Mulcibre fecit Apellem.*"*

As an artist, we have nothing to say about him, save that he arrived at great perfection in the dry style of the school of his time. The picture of the "Two Misers," in Windsor Castle, is the best specimen of his work in this country. He died in 1529.

* "Connubial love made him an Apelles."

JOSEPH JACQUARD,

AND HIS LOOM.

Born 1752—*Died* 1834.

On the 16th August, 1840, the ancient and renowned manufacturing city of Lyons paid a debt of gratitude to one of her citizens, by whose skilful industry and well-applied talent she had been largely enriched and benefited. The scene was one of much stirring interest; an immense concourse of people from the neighbourhood and all the manufacturing population of the town had assembled to witness the ceremony of the inauguration of the statue of Jacquard, the humble weaver, whose career was well known to them all, and who, by general consent, deserved that his fellow-citizens should thus delight to honour his memory. The civil and military authorities assisted on the occasion, and an *éloge*, or discourse in his praise, was pronounced by the mayor of Lyons, to the effect that the name of Jacquard was already famous in both worlds, as the inventor of a machine so simple and inexpensive that it is within reach of the poorest class of workmen, and has introduced a new era in the art of weaving.

The history of this skilful mechanic and worthy man is well adapted to inspire us with respectful admiration for modest, persevering, disinterested labour.

There is something about it of the really heroic, in the best sense; and it shows too, that, in the long run, true merit is discerned, acknowledged, and rewarded.

Born at Lyons, in 1752, Joseph Jacquard was the son of a hand-weaver of brocaded stuffs, whose relatives were poor labourers at the little village of Couson, situated on the right bank of the Soane, some two leagues from Lyons. His father, intending to bring up the boy to his own business, gave him no school instruction of any sort, and little Joseph was his own schoolmaster, and managed by some means to teach himself to read and write. From his childhood he showed a surprising turn for mechanics, and was constantly amusing himself by making little models in wood. He built small houses, towers of churches, and carved miniature furniture; and it was observed that in whatever he made, the proportions were always kept with great exactness. When he was twelve years old, his father placed him in the workshop of a bookbinder, and afterwards with one of the best type-founders of Lyons. Employed in casting type for printing, he showed considerable skill, and, always influenced by his natural turn, made several cutler's tools.

His mother dying, his father soon after took him home, and employed him in his own business, but did not survive many years. Jacquard was thus left an orphan with a very small sum at command, part of which he employed in furnishing a workshop for the fabrication of stuffs. He was not successful in this undertaking, and soon found himself obliged to part with his looms to pay off his debts. In the mean time he had formed an attachment to the daughter of a gunsmith in the town, whom he married not long after. The young couple were tenderly attached to each other, and amidst all the sorrows of poverty and domestic trouble they had to pass through, their mutual affection appears to have remained pure and constant.

The wife is said to have been "a model of patience, of sweet temper, and of industry;" and much need had she for the exercise of all those precious virtues; for her husband, good man, was content if he had but daily bread, and dreamed of nothing but inventions and plans for the improvement of various machinery in the arts of weaving, cutlery, and printing. Unhappily his models and designs did not bring him in a farthing, and it was necessary to live. He sold the cottage which had been his father's, and, little by little, parted with all he possessed. At length he was reduced to such necessity that he was glad to engage himself to work at a limekiln in a neighbouring village, while his wife remained at Lyons, and supported herself by straw-hat-making.

For some years Jacquard lived in obscure penury, nameless, and unknown. When he afterwards emerged into honourable notice, his modesty and natural timidity rendered him slow to speak of his own previous career, and but little is known of his history, or even of the circumstances connected with his great invention. It is certain that, previous to the year 1790, he had conceived the idea of superseding the use of the draw-boy by a moveable pedal, for which invention he obtained a patent in 1801.

Stormy days were those in which Jacquard had to toil and struggle, hard driven as he was, to procure the necessaries of life. His mechanical ideas were interrupted by the sounds of civil strife and deadly warfare. The revolution broke out in Lyons in 1789, and two parties were speedily formed—the one attached to the old *régime*, the other espousing the Jacobin cause. Jacquard eagerly entered into the contest, and, returning to Lyons in 1793, was one of those who defended the city during the memorable siege it sustained against the army of the Convention, when a handful of Lyonese, young and inexperienced in arms, resisted for sixty-six days the combined attacks of famine and a large army of regular troops. The city, being at length compelled to surrender, became the scene of the most lamentable atrocities. The machinery of the principal manufacturers was destroyed, their houses rased to the ground, and themselves led out to execution. Jacquard, who had been one of the foremost in the struggle, was denounced and pursued. He fled, accompanied by his only child, a youth of seventeen. Having effected their escape, they enrolled themselves in the first battalion of the voluntary corps for the department of the Rhone et Loire, and set off to join the army of the Rhine. In a short time, the son fell mortally wounded on the battle-field, and expired in the arms of his father. Overwhelmed by this terrible blow, the unhappy man found his way back to Lyons, where he in vain looked for his poor house—it had been burned to the ground. He knew not what had become of his wife, whom he had not been able to forewarn of his flight, nor to give any subsequent tidings of his movements. At length he found this patient, laborious creature in a garret, still occupied at her old task of platting straw for hats, and he had no better resource than to help her in this manner to earn a scanty pittance.

A considerable time elapsed before Lyons began to recover from the dreadful shock it had sustained; at length, several of its manufacturers, who had taken refuge in Switzerland, Germany, and England, ventured by degrees to return and to resume their occupations. Jacquard, again recurring to his favourite ideas of mechanical improvements, perfected the invention before mentioned, and at the exhibition in 1801, a bronze medal was awarded him for it.

The following year, on occasion of a meeting of the commissioners for the election of a president, attention was directed to the subject of the machinery completed by Jacquard; and some of the members went, accompanied by Carnot, Minister of the Interior, to examine it at the humble dwelling of the inventor. Carnot, who could not comprehend the mechanism, interrogated Jacquard very brusquely; but, unabashed, and with quiet self-possession, he answered the minister in his simple language, and gave such satisfactory replies as fully convinced him of the value of the invention.

In 1804 the large gold medal was awarded him for a machine to make fishing-nets, for which a prize had been offered by the Society of Arts in Paris and in London. So great was his disinterestedness that he did not attempt to secure to himself the monopoly of this invention; and when told of some who were enriching themselves by its means, he would simply reply, "I don't complain: it is enough for me to have been useful to my fellow-citizens, and to deserve their regard."

The merits of Jacquard being now recognized, he was employed at the Conservatory of Arts and Trades, to repair and arrange the machines and models; and subsequently he was placed at an establishment in Lyons for the improvement of various fabrics in manufactures. He now was very desirous to procure the introduction of his two principal inventions into the manufactures of his native city—the machinery for making nets and his famous loom. He was powerfully supported by the influence of a rich manufacturer, who advocated his cause with the municipal council and chamber of commerce of Lyons; and eventually the government authorized them to purchase the patent of the invention, which by this means became public property. Jacquard stipulated, in addition, that he should receive a premium of fifty francs on every machine of his invention. Napoleon, as he signed the necessary order which secured this right to the modest petitioner, exclaimed, "Here, at least, is one who is satisfied with little!"

But Jacquard had now to run the gauntlet with the ignorant prejudice and selfishness of his fellow-workmen, who regarded the new invention with suspicion, thinking it would prove injurious to their interests. They accordingly banded together to prevent its introduction, spoiled the stuffs in order to procure its rejection, and even burned it in the public squares: Jacquard himself was threatened and insulted and on one occasion narrowly escaped being thrown into the Rhone, and was with difficulty rescued from the hands of a furious rabble bent on his destruction.

Terrified and discouraged, he almost despaired of being able to overcome their prejudices; but, happily, some sensible manufacturers persisted in adopting a method by which so many advantages were secured; and before long the results were so obvious that all hastened to follow this example. In the course of a year or two there were 18,000 Jacquard looms going, and their numbers went on increasing. At present this machinery is in use at Lyons, not only for silk but for all varieties of woven stuffs. It was soon introduced into various countries of Europe and America, and the Chinese, overcoming their ancient prejudices, have begun to adopt it.* The successful inventor now

* How great were the benefits resulting from Jacquard's improvements, we are made to realize, when told that the machines formerly in use were inconvenient and complicated in their movements, requiring the labour of numerous hands to keep them in motion. Those employed in this wearisome occupation were principally young women and children, who during the whole day were obliged to remain in painful attitudes, by which their limbs often became deformed—indeed, some contracted mortal diseases.

saw himself loaded with honours. The manufacturers of numerous towns were eager to secure his services for the supervision of the various departments of mechanical trade. The town of Manchester offered him a considerable sum and handsome emoluments to establish himself there; but, refusing all these advantageous and flattering offers, Jacquard preferred to remain in his native city.

There he passed the evening of his days, enjoying, after so many years of toil, struggle, and disappointment, a quiet and honourable repose.

His faithful wife, who had shared his griefs, for a while partook his prosperity, and then sank to the grave. After her loss, Jacquard retired to a small and pretty village a league distant from Lyons, and lived in a small house which had been given him for life. He found occupation and solace during a prolonged old age in cultivating a small garden, and in the humble and devout exercise of his religious duties, and peacefully expired in the month of August, 1834.

The inhabitants of the district testified their respect for his memory in a simple epitaph placed in their church; and his full-length portrait, an admirable likeness, was painted for the corporation of Lyons, and placed in the museum of that city.

RICHARD LENOIR,

THE FRENCH MANUFACTURER.

Born 1762—*Died* 1840.

AMONG the names which rank high as having greatly contributed to the commercial prosperity of France, is that of Richard Lenoir, which will always be remembered with respect and gratitude in all the workshops of the Faubourg St. Antoine.

There is much, both instructive and entertaining, in the early history of this great manufacturer, as well as in the subsequent events of his career. He was not one of "Fortune's favourites" in the world's esteem, and seemed destined by the meanness of his origin to pass a life of labour and obscurity. Born in a small village of Calvados (a department of France in Lower Normandy), he belonged to a family of humble farmers. Like the generality of the children of the peasantry of that district, Richard was sent to school and taught to read and cipher; but his education went no further, and his earliest years were passed in the fields, doing such rough tasks as rustic lads are made to do. Naturally of an active and inventive turn, the lad soon showed symptoms of a decided taste for trade. When he was only twelve years old, he undertook the care of a number of pigeons, and gained a small sum of money by the sale of them. The lord of the manor peremptorily put a stop to that species of traffic, but not before Richard had sold all his pigeons, and, with the forty-two francs they fetched, had procured himself a pair of hobnailed shoes, which he joyfully exchanged for the wooden *sabots* he had hitherto worn in common with his playfellows.

The trade in pigeons was succeeded by one in a handsome breed of dogs, and again he made money. His gains were evident, in the striking difference between his costume and that of the clodhoppers his companions. His next scheme was to go every Wednesday to the weekly market at Villiers le Bocage, the nearest town, where he was intrusted with the keeping of the register of the cattle-market.

At length, when he had attained the age of seventeen, Richard left the home of his boyhood, and directed his steps towards the city of Rouen, with no more than ten francs in his pocket. His first occupation was in the employ of a dealer in printed cottons, named Hermel, who, seeing in him nothing more than a lad deficient in smartness and poorly educated, obliged him to perform various servile offices, and when he remonstrated against such usuage, indignantly dismissed him without a character.

His prospects were now sufficiently dismal, and he was fain to take up with the business of a lemonade-seller, in the hope of earning a sum sufficient to take him to the metropolis. He succeeded in his purpose, and a year afterwards we find this man, who only ten years later was destined to employ thousands of hands and to put in circulation millions of francs, actually a waiter in a coffee-room at Paris, in the Rue St. Denis. He remained in this situation one year, and having realized a capital of 1,000 francs, resolved to go into trade. Throwing aside his white apron, and hiring a room in the sixth story in the Rue St. Honoré, in the neighbourhood of the Piazza, he purchased several pieces of English dimity—at that time a contraband article, and consequently much valued,—and in order to insure a sale, he hawked them about from house to house. Scarcely had six months passed before Richard was in possession of the sum of 6,000 francs.

He thought himself now in a fair way to make his fortune; but, unhappily, he trusted his gains in the hands of an unskilful or faithless agent, and the consequence was, that he speedily lost every farthing, and, still worse, was put in prison for debt.

At length he was set at large, and by the timely assistance of a few friends, who pitied his misfortunes, he obtained a small sum, with which he again entered into business. In the course of two years he had completely re-established his affairs, and realized a small property.

His good fortune encouraged him now to venture on the important step of matrimony; and with honest independence he chose for his wife a young girl of attractive manners and appearance, with unblemished character, but portionless.

He next determined to open a commodious shop in the Rue Française, and was so successful in his speculations that before long he was able to purchase the fine estate of Fayt, near Nemours.

But the evil days of France were close at hand, and already the first intimations of that period so justly called "The Reign of Terror" made the hearts of men tremble. The overthrow of the monarchy, the massacres of the 2nd of September, and the triumph of the anarchists, succeeded each other with fearful rapidity. It was no longer possible for Richard to continue in the capital, and he had the prudence to suspend his commercial operations, which would have tended to endanger rather than to enrich him.

Hastily quitting Paris with his wife, he determined to take refuge in Calvados, and pay a visit to his relatives. His arrival at home seemed a truly providential circumstance. Hardly had he crossed his father's threshold, when bailiffs presented themselves to arrest the old man. He had gone bail for a tax-gatherer, who had absconded, carrying away the funds with him. Richard and his wife had come on foot from Caen, and their appearance gave no indication of their prosperous circumstances. Great, therefore, was the surprise when, drawing out a purse of gold, he hastened to satisfy the demands of these unwelcome intruders, and flung his arms around his mother's neck. Verily, the ten francs, with which he had taken his departure ten years before, had yielded an abundant increase!

At the end of a few months Robespierre and his accomplices had reaped the due reward of their horrid deeds, and their fall had restored hope and confidence to trade. The young couple were now at liberty to return to Paris, where Richard soon added to his former trade that of lapidary, which he found exceedingly profitable.

It was about 1797 that chance threw him into contact with a young merchant named Lenoir Dufresne. Both had resolved to buy the same bale of English goods. Pleased with each other, they agreed to share the purchase together, and soon after entered into a partnership, which lasted till the death of Lenoir. The two men were admirably suited. Lenoir was intelligent, patient, and circumspect. Richard, more enterprising, was bold in his projects, and resolute in carrying them out. Their united energies proved eminently successful. Their establishment attracted crowds of purchasers, and when, after fourteen months, they made their inventory, they found the 6,000 francs they had invested in the business had produced a return of 112,000 francs. Their great profit was upon English goods.

"The time had now come," says one of Richard's biographers, "for him to become himself the manufacturer of cotton stuffs, in which he had so long speculated with so much success."

It is said his resolution was finally decided by this chance: — One day, during his partner's absence, he amused himself with ravelling the threads of some

English goods. He weighed these threads, and ascertained that a piece of eight yards in length, and worth eighty francs, only weighed eight pounds, and could only have been valued at twelve francs in its original state—consequently sixty-eight francs remained for the working up. This was a new light on the subject.

There were many difficulties to encounter; but commercial enterprise sufficed to overcome them. He set himself to the task. His first two looms were set up in a public-house in the Rue Bellefon , and dimity similar to the English was woven. An English prisoner named Brown gave the necessary instructions to some French workmen, and Lenoir found out the method of figuring it. A spinning-factory was now requisite to the perfection of the new art. Richard, by the assistance of another Englishman (Brownwell), had twenty-two mule-jennies constructed, with carding-machines and trundles. These he established in a large house in the Rue de Thorigny. The stuffs sold well and rapidly, for they were believed to be of English manufacture.

In want of space for his rapidly-increasing machinery, and under the daily necessity of procuring more workmen, Richard, confiding in the protection of the first consul, Bonaparte, by a bold stroke ventured to take possession of the deserted buildings known as the Convent of Bon Secours. Causing the vast apartments to be repaired with the speed of enchantment, he filled them with his workmen; and when one of the government commissioners was on the point of ejecting these busy workers, Napoleon, being informed of the facts, personally visited the establishment, and expressed his approbation of the activity visible in every department. Unable, at first, to appreciate the merits of Richard's enterprise, he asked why he undertook to manufacture the goods, when he could make a certain profit by the sale of the English goods. "The interest of my country is my main object," was the reply; "the desire to get rid of a burdensome impost paid to England, and of giving employment and bread to some thousands of families." The first consul testified his satisfaction by giving the two partners permission to occupy the former convent of Trênelle, situated opposite to that of Bon Secours.

Thus patronized, this new branch of trade flourished to a surprising extent, and enormous profits were reaped, amounting, it was said, to 40,000 francs a month. Encouraged by this unparalleled success, our manufacturers redoubled their activity in extending their labours. Before long 300 looms were established in various villages of Picardy; forty in Alençon, 100 mule-jennies, and more than 200 weavers' looms in the abbey of St. Martin, near Luzarches. An arrangement was made by them for giving employment to all the women who were in gaol at Alençon.

After the death of Lenoir, in 1806,—which was an occasion of great sorrow to all the poor of the Faubourg St. Antoine, — Richard (now universally known by the name of Lenoir, which he assumed in compliance with the desire of his dying partner) continued his business with undiminished energy. He introduced spinning-factories at Caen and l'Aigle, and a cotton-printing establishment at Chantilly, and undertook the cultivation of cotton, which he commenced successfully at Naples. He was now at the summit of his prosperity. In 1810 the new tax laid upon cotton struck a heavy blow at his establishments, and he was involved in great difficulties. Napoleon came to his assistance, and obliged the government to advance him the sum of 1,500,000 francs, and he exchanged his cotton mills for woollen ones. Had this great manufacturer solely consulted his own interests, he might now have withdrawn with safety to himself, in possession of a sufficient income; but he looked on his workmen as his children, and could not leave them without work, a prey to want and misery. He struggled on against an adverse legislation for a while; but difficulties increased upon him, and the union of France with Holland, which all at once overstocked the French markets with English produce, and, finally, the law of the 25th of April, which entirely suppressed the former taxes upon foreign produce, were the precursors of heavy calamities to the French manufacturers. This active and enterprising man, who, at a time by no means prosperous, had employed 20,000 workmen, was now completely ruined.

Richard Lenoir had received the Cross of Honour from the hands of the emperor himself. During his disasters of 1813, Napoleon, appreciating his influence in the Faubourg St. Antoine, made him colonel of the 8th legion of the national guard of Paris. Each of his workmen became a soldier; he clothed and exercised them, and inspired them with that blind devotion he himself felt for Napoleon. On the 8th of January, 1814, he distinguished himself in the defence of the capital, no less by his courage than by the generous humanity he evinced in succouring the wounded, often at his own expense, always to the injury of his neglected manufactures.

On the restoration of the Bourbons, in 1815, the name of this honourable citizen was on the list of proscription and exile; but he applied personally to the Russian emperor, Alexander, by whom he was affably received, and through whose influence the sentence against him was rescinded.

He remained, therefore, in his native land; but reduced to poverty, forgotten, and almost unknown, he died in Paris, on the 12th of October, 1840, at the age of seventy-eight. His funeral was without pomp, but not without honour. The procession, leaving the house of death in the Faubourg Montmartre, consisted of an immense concourse of mechanics, and received new additions at every step. Arrived at the the manufactory of Bon Secours, they paused, in accordance with the wishes of Lenoir himself, who had expressed a desire to be carried thither after his death, and to be, for the last time, surrounded by those to whom he had been so fond a master. In the centre of the magnificent building, the workmen had raised a monument combining simplicity with grandeur. Above the bust of Richard Lenoir stood the statue of Napoleon; on the front of the pedestal were inscribed these words:—"*The Emperor lends* 1,500,000 *francs to Richard Lenoir.*" On the other side—"*Richard Lenoir marches to the defence of Paris at the head of* 20,000 *united workmen.*"

OBERKAMPF,

AND CALICO-PRINTING IN FRANCE.

Born 1738—*Died* 1815.

FEW persons have any idea of the variety of operations which cotton has to undergo before it is fit for use, nor think that, in order to produce the dress of a poor peasant-girl, the resources of chemistry, taste, and mechanical skill are all laid under contribution. Most multifarious and delicate are the processes requisite in calico-printing, which has been styled "the most interesting, curious, and refined of all the chemical arts."

So intricate and difficult a process would seem to be characteristic of the scientific refinement of these later days, and yet it was known to the ancient Hindus and Egyptians. The celebrated Roman naturalist, Pliny, describes it with much precision. He says, "Robes and white veils are painted in Egypt in a wonderful way, being first imbued, not with dyes, but with dye-absorbing drugs, by which they appear to be unaltered; but when plunged for a little in a cauldron of the boiling stuff, they are found to be painted. Since there is only one colour in the cauldron, it is marvellous to see many colours imparted to the robe, in consequence of the modifying agency of the drug.* Nor can the dye be washed out. Thus the cauldron, which would of itself undoubtedly confuse the colours of cloths previously dyed, is made to impart several dyes from a single one, painting while it boils."

In India, where manufacturing processes have probably suffered little changes in the course of three thousand years, not only is the art of using these drugs well known, but that of applying resist-pastes, in order to preserve the cloth from the action of the dye-bath in any desired figures or spots. In the Industrial Society of Mühlhausen (a town of great celebrity in calico-printing) may be seen specimens, not only of modern Indian calicoes in the preparation state, covered with wax in places, to serve as a resist to the indigo dye, but of ancient styles of pencilled cloths, which had been the work of princesses, covered with figures of such complexity as could not be made without a very tedious and costly education, beyond the reach of ordinary artisans. Among other curiosities, the counterpane of a state bed is shown, six yards long and three broad, which must have taken a lifetime to execute, on their plan of applying the melted wax with a pencil.

English calicoes and muslins, now among the most important of our textile products, are the fruit of

* Thus, if white calico be impressed with the drug of acetate of alumina in one set of lines, with that of acetate of iron in a second, and with a mixture of the two in a third,—on being exposed to the madder-bath for a proper time, it will become permanently printed in red, black, and chocolate stripes.

mechanical improvements, and quite of modern date. The art was not introduced into this country until the latter end of the seventeeth century, and encountered at the outset the keenest hostility from the silk and woollen manufacturers; nor were the restrictions upon it wholly removed till the year 1831, when they were finally repealed, and the business left to its natural development. In France the same restrictions were long enforced, and a severe prohibition forbade the importation of printed calicoes and chintzes from other countries. There, as here, the interests of hemp, flax, and silk manufactures were alleged against it. But at length a man of indomitable perseverance and first-rate artistic skill triumphed over all obstacles, and introduced this branch of industry, which soon spread over all France, and was attended with great prosperity.

This man was Christopher Oberkampf, who was born at Weissenburg, in Franconia, in 1738. The lad served an apprenticeship to his father, in the manufacture of printed calicoes; the latter, an ingenious, worthy, and industrious man, after having tried without success to settle in various towns of Germany, had finally established a manufactory at Arau, in Switzerland, where he was rewarded with the rights of citizenship, in return for his energetic efforts in favour of his valuable art. Under so skilful a master the young man acquired much valuable information, which afterwards gained him both fortune and fame.

At that time, as we have said, printed calicoes and

chintzes were prohibited in France, and were sold at very high prices.

It was reserved for Oberkampf, a stranger youth, poor and unbefriended, hardly able to speak in French, an adherent of a faith prohibited by the laws of France (he was a Lutheran), to establish the first manufactory of these fabrics, and thus to render such services to his adopted country as secured to him universal admiration and gratitude.

Ambitious to emulate his father's successful career, he conceived the project of founding a manufactory in France; and for that purpose left his home, and set out for Paris, carrying with him all his savings, which amounted to no more than 600 francs. He was then only nineteen years of age. After many and urgent solicitations, he, at length, obtained permission to form an establishment, and he lost no time in setting to work.

He remarked, in the neighbourhood of Versailles, a waste tract of land, situated in the valley of Jouy; a wide-spreading marsh made this spot extremely unwholesome, but he knew that well-directed labour would soon avail to drain and fertilize it, and render it agreeable and salubrious. He fixed on this as the ground for his experiment. At first, entirely dependent on his own resources, Oberkampf lived alone, in a small cottage belonging to one of the peasants. Step by step he took his measures, and proceeded to carry out his designs. He had to combat the prejudices of the neighbouring proprietors, the ill-directed zeal of some of the authorities, and the suspicions of government; but an indomitable perseverance and prodigious activity, combined with resolute will, overcame all obstacles. By degrees he obtained assistants, and inspired them with confidence in his own views, and they carried into execution the measures he devised. He was himself designer, printer, and painter—all in one; but, by-and-by, his solitary residence was peopled in a surprising manner. He undertook the instruction of apprentices and pupils; he produced articles of unprecedented elegance and beauty, and no sooner did they make their appearance in the market than the ingenious fabricator found himself the object of interest and curiosity. The inhabitants of the capital and the court hastened to purchase these unequalled productions; and the fair ladies eagerly adopted the graceful *robes de matin* which the taste and skill of the young manufacturer offered them. In short, his goods became "the rage," and their fame spread far and wide, so that, before long, they found ready sale in London as well as in Paris.

In the course of time the establishment at Jouy became a large and flourishing manufacture, where upwards of a thousand men were employed.

Oberkampf was not the man to rest satisfied because success had crowned his efforts; he lost no opportunity for introducing new improvements, and for extending his knowledge. His agents were sent into England and Germany, and even into the East, whence they procured him varied information relative to the secrets of his art, and more especially in dyeing those rich colours for which the manufactures of India and Persia are so renowned. He succeeded by these means in gaining great perfection, and combined beauty of design with brilliant hues. His window-blinds, coloured and drawn after the style of the old-fashioned church windows, were greatly admired; and, by admitting the light with the effect of a transparency, were very effective.

From year to year his establishment went on increasing in prosperity, and its founder triumphed completely over the various obstacles which prejudice and self-interest had opposed to his progress. By the exhibition of his manufactures, he eventually succeeded in releasing France from the heavy imposts paid to foreign countries; and the great manufacturing cities of the land, Rouen, Lyons, Le Beaujolois, &c., were at length convinced that the man who, by his labours, had opened for their products a vast and growing market, could not be inimical to their interests.

Before the breaking out of the French Revolution, Oberkampf was in the enjoyment of considerable renown. Louis XVI., anxious to recompense the man who created for his countrymen so important a branch of industry, gave him letters of nobility, couched in the most flattering terms; but he had the modesty and good sense to refuse an honour which would have rendered him the object of so much envy. During the Reign of Terror, which followed shortly after, he narrowly escaped banishment; it was even a question whether he should not be put to death! Napoleon, who neglected nothing which tended to promote the prosperity of his empire, did not overlook this remarkable man. When he visited the Jouy manufactory, he took the cross from his own breast, and placed it upon that of Oberkampf, whom he addressed in the most eulogistic terms: "You," said he, "Seïgneur de Jouy, carry on, as I do, a spirited warfare against England; you oppose her by your industry; I, by force of arms. I must, however, confess," he added, "that your mode of warfare is preferable to mine."

At that very time Oberkampf was endeavouring to learn the English method of spinning and weaving cotton, in which he was successful; for he established the spinning-mill at Essone, which was the first of the kind introduced into France.

In 1790 the council-general of the department of Oise, in consideration of Oberkampf's services, wished to erect a statue in honour of him; but he, with the same modesty which caused him to decline Louis XVI.'s offer of nobility, would not consent to it. Under the empire he also refused the dignity of senator offered him by Napoleon.

The last days of Oberkampf were embittered by grief. This was in 1815; the ravages of war, which then overran France, did not spare the peaceful valley of Jouy. It was laid waste by the tread of the foreign invader, and its venerable patriarch mourned as he witnessed the desolation and suffering around him. Now, instead of the hum of busy voices and the scenes of prosperous industry, he heard only the mournful silence of poverty and despair, exchanged for the life and abundance which his own exertions had introduced into that much-loved spot. His workshops were closed, and the workmen who had served him for sixty-one years now asked in vain for employment and for bread. "This spectacle kills me," exclaimed the venerable old man; nor did he long endure it. He expired in the month of October, 1815, leaving behind him (says one of his biographers) "an almost pious veneration cherished in the hearts of all who had known him."

The branch of industry which Oberkampf originated prospered greatly in France. "Numerous establishments," says M. Foucaud, "have been formed upon the plan of that at Jouy. The workmen employed in them are estimated at from 200,000 to 300,000. From a raw material of the value of 60,000,000 francs is gained a profit of 240,000,000 francs. At present the richest and most beautiful designs are printed on cotton; three or four colours are combined, presenting a beautifully shaded appearance. The exportation of printed calicoes has been an important part of French commerce, this material being used for bed and window curtains, coverings for divans, sofas, armchairs, &c. &c.; and all is due to Oberkampf."

BERNARD PALISSY.

Born 1500—*Died* 1589.

"Then I went down to the potter's house, and behold! he wrought a work on the wheels."

WORKING in earth, or the art of the potter, is of the greatest antiquity, and its history is full of interest. Were we to go back to the days of the old Egyptians, we might recall the sorrows of the Israelites in the house of their bondage, and the remembrances connected with their labours in the field, when they toiled to make bricks for their cruel task-masters; and as we dwelt on this record of the remote past, how would our hearts burn within us! Or if, glancing over the history of mankind, we examined the memorials of bygone generations, our attention would often be called to "the art of the potter"—that art "without which how many others would be useless, if not altogether lost." The uses of clay are numerous and great; but we are not about to speak of them. Our purpose is to give the reader a short sketch of the life of Palissy, who has been called in these modern times "the prince of potters." He is indeed a worthy model to be offered to the sympathy and imitation of working men; and, happily, we have, from his own pen, the record of his struggles in the acquisition of that art upon which his reputation is founded.

Bernard Palissy P. 106

Of his early days, no more is known than the little which can be gathered from his occasional allusions to them in a treatise which he wrote on the art of pottery. It appears he was born at the beginning of the sixteenth century, in the diocese of Agen ; his parents were poor, and he received in his childhood no more than a peasant's education, except that he learned to draw and paint on glass—his father being, probably, a glass-worker. "I have had no other books," said he, "than heaven and earth, which are open to all." Bernard, however, learned to read and write, and the business of a glass-painter requiring that he should copy plans and drawings, he acquired some knowledge of drawing and surveying, which he afterwards turned to excellent account. About the age of eighteen, he quitted his native hamlet, and went to make his way in the world as best he might.

Some years passed before he finally settled in the town of Saintes, it is supposed about 1538. During the intervening time he had wandered about the principal provinces of France, occasionally remaining for months, or even years, in a town where he found employment. He had seen with an observing eye the ways of men, and studied with care the works of art and monuments of antiquity that fell under his notice, cultivating the talents which nature had given him. Above all, his great love for natural history had made him a keen and intelligent student of that marvellous book which God has spread open to show forth His praises, and declare His glory to the children of men.

The attention of Palissy was particularly directed to the study of minerals and earths; and he had acquired some knowledge of chemistry—a science then but in its infancy; in short, he had learned many things, and his mind was stored with knowledge, gathered up as material for future use; but his working-days were yet to come.

Having become "a family man," Palissy was no longer free to wander about, living as he could, "from hand to mouth,"—to use an old saying of some significance. He settled himself in a cottage at Saintes, a small and ancient town in the south-west of France, and here, for a year or two, he gained a decent living for himself, his wife, and babes, by glass-painting and surveying.

And now an incident occurred which he thus tells in the treatise already spoken of. "There was shown me an earthen cup, turned and enamelled with so much beauty that, from that time, I began to think if I could discover how to make enamels, I might make earthen vessels and other things very prettily, because God had gifted me with some knowledge of drawing." At that time Palissy knew nothing of the art of pottery, and there was no man in France who could do enamelling; but, "regardless of the fact that I had no knowledge of clays," he continues, "I began to seek for the enamels as a man gropes in the dark." Accordingly, he set to work and pounded all the substances he supposed likely to serve his purpose; he purchased drugs, bought earthen pots, and built a furnace, all to the neglect of his ordinary business, and at considerable expense. He foresaw the task would prove a difficult one, and that sacrifices must be made; but he heeded not poverty and pain in searching, provided he might at length succeed. What occasioned him most anxiety, and proved the greatest obstacle to his progress, was the fact that "he was intrusted with a wife and children," which rendered it impossible for him to go and learn the rudiments of the art in some shop or pottery, and he had no means for engaging servants to help him.

The first experiment proved a total failure; for want of experience he committed the grossest blunders, and reaped only disappointment as the fruit of much time, labour, and money.

Month after month he persevered, "every day pounding and grinding new materials, and consuming wood and time." It was ruinous work, and he assures us that he "fooled away in this manner several years with sorrow and sighs." The time was not, in reality, wasted; for, as has been truly said, "when men grope in the dark, it is by touching on all sides upon what they do not seek that they at length find what they desire." His narrow means, however, would not suffer him continually to go on with this profitless labour, and he determined to try a new plan, and to send the chemicals he was testing to the kiln of some potter to be burnt, thus avoiding the most expensive part of the process—the building of furnaces, and the watching and feeding them with fuel. He describes most minutely his proceedings, and tells how his "trial-pieces" all came from the baking "good for nothing," and procured him "nothing but shame and loss." Great was his disappointment, and, as he was totally ignorant of the cause of the failure, he blamed the materials, while, in reality, the fire used by the potters was not hot enough to melt the glaze. And so . . . What must he do? There was to his earnest and intent spirit no choice but "to begin afresh," which he accordingly did—"and so continued to do several times, always with great cost, loss of time, confusion, and sorrow."

Meantime the family of this poor man kept pace in increase with his difficulties. His home wants had multiplied, and there were wan cheeks and hungry mouths around his board. It was evident there must be a truce for the time to this profitless work, and accordingly he tells us, in the simplicity of his heart, that, "seeing he could not in this way come at his intention, he took relaxation for a time, occupying himself in his art of painting and glass-working, and behaved as though he were not zealous any more to dive into the secret of enamels."

A prosperous time ensued for the little household. In May, 1543, Palissy received a very profitable commission "to map the salt-marshes in the district of Saintonge." From the account he has given of the marsh district, it is evident that no slight labour was required accurately to survey it. Hard at work during the dry season of summer, he was busily occupied in mapping the towns and villages in the winter-time, when the marshes were all under water. He brought his work to a close some time in the succeeding year, and then, "when the commission was ended, and I found myself supplied with a little money," says our enthusiast, "I resumed my affection for pursuing the search of the enamels."

The first act he mentions as commencing this second crusade of discovery was apparently so unreasonable as to alarm any one. "I broke about three dozen earthen pots, all of them new." His home-made furnaces had failed, and the potters' furnaces had also failed, not being hot enough; he therefore resolved to try the furnaces used by glass-workers, and returned to his old method of strewing his broken bits of pottery with different chemical mixtures; for, by covering three separate fragments with each compound he thought likely to melt into a white enamel, Palissy hoped to give himself a fair chance of success in hitting upon the discovery. He sent this batch of trial-pieces to the glass-house, and for the first time he perceived that some of his compounds had begun to melt. "This little symptom (how small a ray of hope!) caused me to work on two years longer, during all which time I did nothing but come and go between my house and the adjacent glass-houses, aiming to succeed in my object."

Think of these two additional years of zealous, toilsome labour, without any visible result, and shall we not marvel at the persevering, indomitable energy of this man?

Again the urgent cares of home compelled him to desist; and he therefore determined, with a heavy heart, on sending one last batch to the furnace, and if that should prove a failure, he would yield to stern necessity, and devote himself wholly to his early trade.

This closing effort he would have to be a strenuous one, so he broke more pots than ever, purchased a great variety of drugs, and made no fewer than 300 different chemical mixtures, each of which might possibly be found to contain the long-desired substance.

It was a turning-point in his history when, his trial-pieces being all put into the furnace, he sat down there, beside the furnace-mouth, to wait the result, anxious and intent. During four hours he waited—at length the furnace was opened, and his pieces drawn out; on one of them the material was melted, and that piece, when cool, "turned out white and polished—a white enamel, singularly beautiful, which caused him such joy as made him think he had become a new creature."

He now believed that his troubles were over; but, in truth, they were only begun, for he had yet to turn the knowledge he had acquired with so much toil and pain to practical advantage. The success of this trial made him at once give up his intention of returning to his old business, and he set himself without delay to work. He had found that a furnace like that of the glass-makers would serve his purpose; he must, therefore, build such a one for himself; and, as he could not afford to pay for help, he had to be his own mason and bricklayer. Then came the labour of grinding the materials for the enamel, and of heating the furnace, and, when all was done, it proved vain, for the enamel would not melt, and he was "like a man in desperation." Although "quite stupefied with labour," he still persisted, however, and began his work afresh; he knew how much depended on perseverance now, and very touchingly does he relate the position into which he had been brought. Having for more than three weeks been imprisoned in an outhouse with his furnace, which he was obliged to watch night and day, he was overtaken by a new misfortune. His supply of fuel ran short, and he had none at hand. "Thus the wood having failed me," he says, "I was forced to burn the palings which surrounded my garden, and when they were burnt, I was forced to burn also the tables and flooring of my house, to cause the melting of the composition. I suffered an anguish I cannot speak; for I was quite exhausted, and dried up by the heat of the furnace; it was more than a month since my shirt had been dry upon me; and, further to distress me, I was the object of mockery, and even those from whom solace was due, ran crying through the town that I was burning my floors, so that I was regarded as a madman."

We cannot be surprised that such a verdict should be pronounced by those who saw only the melancholy results of so many years' labour and suffering; and if his poor wife and hungry children became impatient, and complained with loud outcry, who among us can cast a stone at them, if we do but place ourselves, in imagination, in similar circumstances?

Yet, plunged as he was in disaster, Bernard Palissy had reason to be sure that he had discovered the profitable art, of which for six or seven years he had been in search. Family and friends pronounced him mad; but he had gained the knowledge he desired, and now the difficulty that remained was to make a profitable use of it. Overwhelmed with poverty, he struggled on through several more long years before he attained superior skill. He must have had great strength of body to endure, in addition to privation and distress, the intense toil to which he submitted himself in the prosecution of his struggles. Even his powerful frame bore at length strong marks of the contest; for he tells us, "I was for the space of ten years so wasted in my person, that there was no form nor prominence of muscle on my arms or legs. . . . . Often I walked about the fields of Saintes, considering my miseries and weariness, and above all things, that in my own house I could have no repose, and was despised and mocked by all. Still I blundered on; and when I had learned to guard against one difficulty, then came another of which I had not thought. At last I found means to make several vessels of different enamels, intermixed in the manner of jasper. That fed me for several years. When afterwards I had discovered how to make my rustic pieces, I was in greater trouble and vexation even than before; for my enamels turned out some beautiful, others ill-melted, others burnt, because they were composed of different materials that were fusible in different degrees—the green of the lizards was burnt before the colour of the serpents was melted, and the colours of the serpents, lobsters, tortoises, and crabs were melted before the white had attained any beauty. All these defects caused me so much labour and heaviness of spirit, that before I could render my enamels fusible at the same degree of heat, I thought I should be at the door of my sepulchre."

Palissy founded his reputation on the manufacture of what he called "rustic pieces;" and the title which he took for himself was that of "Worker in Earth, and Inventor of Rustic Figulines" (or small modellings). These were, in fact, accurate models from life of wild animals, reptiles, plants, and other objects, tastefully combined as ornaments, and inwrought with the texture of the vessel. As much a naturalist as a potter, he delighted to imitate upon his ware the bright colours and elegant forms of leaves, flowers, and living creatures; and Mr. Marryatt, a connoisseur in porcelain and fancy pottery, says of the Palissy ware:—"The natural objects which are placed upon this *faïence* are very true in form and colour; for, with the exception of certain leaves, they were all moulded from nature. The choice he has made shows that this potter was a skilful naturalist; for the fossil shells with which he has ornamented his different pieces are the tertiary shells of the Paris basin, and their species can be clearly recognised. The fish are those of the

Seine; the reptiles and plants, of the environs of Paris. There is no foreign natural production to be seen on his ware."*

And now, having seen our illustrious potter thus toiling and suffering to acquire the skill which was to make him immortal in the history of art, we must pause for awhile to consider him in another aspect. How diligently he wrought, how lovingly he studied, how indomitably he persevered, we have seen. What was the secret source of so much activity and such surprising self-denial? Let him speak for himself:—"I have found nothing better," he says (in the preface to one of his treatises) "than to observe the counsel of God, His edicts, statutes, and ordinances; and in regard to His will, I have seen that He has commanded His followers to eat bread by the labour of their bodies, and to multiply the talents which He has committed to them."

In these few words we have the clue to his life's history. The idea which he solemnly and repeatedly recurred to in all his daily life, the "mainspring of his intellectual machinery," was the parable of the talents—the duty of every man placed in the world to see how he may best turn his powers to account, and do the utmost good of which his mind is capable.

It was religious principle which, aiding and engthening his natural activity of spirit, forced m to pursue with unwearying energy the upward

* The celebrated Buffon pronounced Palissy to be "so great a naturalist as Nature only can produce."

path. He laboured with the conviction that the eye of God was upon him; and when he desired rest and refreshment he walked abroad and communed with the earth and sky; for he said, "It is a thing just before God, and a great recreation to those who will contemplate admiringly the wondrous works of Nature, glorifying God, and recognising Him in His marvels." Everywhere in his writings Palissy shows a close and reverent acquaintance with the Bible. His quaint and cheerful temper, his artless and vivacious spirit, are united to a solemn religious feeling.

The times in which he lived were stormy and evil; and Palissy, who had embraced the religious views of the Huguenots (or Protestants of France) knew well that at any time he might be called upon to suffer and to die for his faith. But, as he hesitated not to face poverty and reproach in the pursuit of his calling, so he was willing to hazard his life for the cause of Christ Jesus his Lord. In the days of his deepest trouble, when he was struggling, as we have seen, he found consolation in studying the Scripture daily with one poor companion; and these two, having taken counsel together, found out some four or five "simple and unlearned men" like themselves, who assembled "one Sunday, in the morning," for the purpose of holding religious worship. Palissy took the lead, and "propounded to them the parable of the talents, and many other such texts," and then exhorted them that it was the duty of all people to speak of God's ordinances and statutes, and that his auditors should do as he was doing." They accordingly agreed to meet and make exhortations weekly, on Sabbath-days; and "that was the beginning of the reformed Church of the town of Saintes." Of the commencement, prosperity, and sufferings of this Christian community, Palissy has given a short narrative, full of deep and earnest feeling and worthy to form a chapter in a new Book of Martyrs. His heart overflowed as he penned the record; and well it might, for he was a sharer in the joys and sorrows, and partook of the deep trials he described.

As we pursue our narrative, we shall have melancholy proof that in France, during the sixteenth century, men could not follow the dictates of their own consciences without incurring peril of the most fearful penalties.

In the meanwhile, Palissy was prospering in his art. His beautiful designs in pottery, completed with much labour, sold at a price which only the wealthy could afford to pay; and men of rank and influence becoming acquainted with his skill, readily supplied him with commissions.

The celebrated Constable Montmorenci who, during a considerable part of his life, stood first in court favour, and possessed immense wealth, was at that time occupied in the adornment of his famous Chateau d'Ecouen, about four leagues from Paris; and being made acquainted with the unique skill of Palissy, employed him in some of the encaustic decorations of that mansion, and constituted himself the head patron of the man who had thus succeeded in stamping his genius on clay. Undoubtedly this lofty patronage sufficed to establish our artist's worldly prospects. A man who had been entrusted to assist in the embellishment of one of the most famous architectural works of his time would be sure to have plenty of commissions from a host of gentry who had castles to build or improve.

Happily engaged in such work, and far removed from the old days of solitary toil, he had now two sons assisting in the labours of the well-appointed workshop. All was prosperous in worldly matters; but the troubles that were now beginning to overwhelm the land soon were felt at Saintes. Indeed every town in France was filled with the riot of contending factions, and before long the capital of Saintonge was assailed and taken by a hostile leader, who treated with savage cruelty all the adherents of the reformed party. A terrible scene followed, and the workshop of Palissy was broken into by a rude rabble, himself compelled to hide in a corner, and at length, when discovered, dragged, under the shadow of night, to a dungeon at Bordeaux.

Had he not acquired his secret as a potter, had not his death involved the extinction of a valuable and unique ornamental art, beyond doubt he would in that year—1562—have perished upon the gallows. He was only saved by the prompt interference of the King's lieutenant in Saintes, who immediately bestirred himself, and communicated to Montmorenci the imminent peril that threatened his ingenious workman. The Constable applied to the Queen-Mother, Catherine de Medicis, then regent, to protect a clever artist, whose skill might be turned to good account in her service. An edict was accordingly issued in the king's name, appointing Palissy inventor of rustic figulines to the Queen and the Constable, and thus, saved from the threatened death, he was free to return to his home, where he quietly resumed his occupation in the half-depopulated town of Saintes. He did not long continue there, as his position in a remote province became very inconvenient, when his chief employers were the great men of the court. He therefore removed to Paris, and established his workshop in the neighbourhood of the Tuileries. During the ten years that followed his removal to the French capital, Palissy—familiarly called "Bernard of the Tuileries"—continued to labour at his vocation; and, his taste being now assisted by the study of the best works of art collected in the metropolis, he was able far to surpass his former efforts in the production of elegant and rich designs.

Very few traces of his larger works, designed for garden architecture, now remain; but his smaller productions, consisting of statuettes, elegant groups, vases, cups, plates, dishes, rustic basins, and many others moulded into beautiful forms, enamelled and painted, still remain, and fetch high prices as works of taste in our day. Some are covered with modellings, exquisitely coloured, of fruit, shells, fishes, and reptiles. Others are adorned with coloured pictures, in delicate bas-relief, of subjects taken from Holy Writ or from mythology. The colours used by Palissy were, commonly, bright tints of yellow, blue, or grey; he used also, though less frequently, green, violet, and brown.

Mr. Marryat, in his "History of Pottery and Porcelain," says that the most extensive and complete collection of Palissy ware is in the Royal Museum of the Louvre and in the Hotel de Cluny. "These magnificent specimens were eagerly bought up by the French government, from a just appreciation of the merits of their talented and much-persecuted countryman."

At the same time that he exercised his skill as an artist, Palissy was actively pursuing his studies as a naturalist and philosopher among the men of taste and learning with whom he was now able to live in constant intercourse.

Unmolested amid the outbreaks of civil war, and unharmed even amid the terrors of the massacre of St. Bartholomew, he continued, year after year, quietly pursuing his way, no man interrupting him. He became known, in the latter period of his life, as a man of science and a collector of natural curiosities, and formed a cabinet of natural history, the first ever seen in Paris. There he opened a course of lectures, which were attended by the first men of the day, who listened with interest while the vigorous old man poured out the lessons he had learned by the road sides, on the sea shore, and among the mountains.

In our own times, such men as Buffon, Haller, and Jussieu, have spoken with admiration of the wisdom and surprising sagacity evinced in his works, which, undoubtedly, entitle him to a very high rank among the philosophers of the sixteenth century.

The last scene in the history of Palissy cannot fail to call forth our warmest emotions of admiration and painful sympathy. He had reached an age considerably beyond the usual span of mortal life, when, during the fifth civil war under Henry III., he was committed to the terrible prison of the Bastille, in consequence of a decree prohibiting the future exercise of the reformed religion, on pain of death. He was well known to be a Huguenot; and no royal edict could alter his convictions, nor induce him to deny the faith which he held dearer than life.

As an ancient servant of his mother, the king was unwilling to see this good and venerable man perish at the stake, and he went one day to the place in which Palissy was incarcerated, and tried to shake his resolution. "I have been compelled, my good man," he said, "in spite of myself, to imprison you, pressed as I am by the Guise party and my own people; nor can I prevent them putting you to death, unless you will be converted." "Sire," replied the noble-hearted old man, "you tell me you pity me; it is for me to pity you who have said, 'I am compelled.' Those are not the words of a king. The Guises, joined to all your people, shall never compel me. I know how to die."

Palissy remained four years enclosed within those prison walls, his life being spared through the interposition of some of his exalted patrons and friends. The wretched monarch, Henry III., perished by the hand of an assassin, in the year 1589. That same year Palissy the Potter died in the Bastille.

JOHN RENNIE.

Born 1761—*Died* 1821.

WHO, that stands on Waterloo bridge and admires that fine structure, which foreigners admit has no parallel in Europe for its magnitude, beauty, and solidity, does not reverence the genius of its great architect, John Rennie?

This distinguished mechanician, architect, and civil engineer—for he excelled in these three kindred branches of art—was born on the 7th June, 1761, at Phantassie, in the parish of Prestonkirk, East Lothian. His father was a respectable farmer there, and died in 1766, leaving a widow and nine children, of whom John was the youngest. The little fellow was sent to the village-school, and, as it not unfrequently happens, that some trivial circumstance in early life gives a bent to the pursuits, and thus influences the future career of the man, so it was in his case.

In order to go from his mother's house to the school, it was necessary to cross a brook, over which the usual passage was by a rustic bridge of stepping-stones; but, in the winter season, when the waters were swollen, the stream became impassable, except by means of a boat, which was kept at the workshop of Mr. Andrew Meikle, an ingenious mechanic, well known in Scotland as the inventor of the threshing machine and many improvements in agricultural implements. In this way it chanced that the young Rennie had frequent opportunities for passing through the workshop and watching the proceedings of the men as they pursued their avocation. So greatly was he interested in these things, that every spare hour and all his holidays were sure to find him at his post, examining the various operations in progress. The delight he thus evinced drew the attention of the master and workmen, who were in the habit of indulging the boy with their tools, and showing him their various uses. His evenings were chiefly employed in imitating those models which had particularly attracted his attention in the workshop; and it is said, that when little more than ten years old, he had constructed the model of a windmill, a pile-engine, and a steam-engine. Thus "the boy was father to the man." At the age of twelve years, he entreated permission to leave the school, as he deemed the master incompetent to give him any further instructions. His request was granted, and in compliance with his desire he was placed with his friend, Mr. Meikle, and remained for about two years in his employ. At the end of that time, his mind expanding with his growth, he became desirous of further mental education, and therefore, determined to place himself under the tuition of Mr. Gibson, teacher of mathematics at Dunbar. His progress, at the end of two or three years' application, was such, that it was prophesied he would, at no distant period, prove an honour to his country, and Mr. Gibson being promoted to the academy at Perth, earnestly recommended him as his successor. The bent of his genius, however, lay in a different direction, and after a very short essay at school-keeping, he returned to his family, occasionally visiting and assisting his old friend and master, Mr. Meikle, but mostly applying himself to the study of elementary mechanics, and practising himself in the art of drawing machinery, and the different objects which belong to practical architecture.

His first essay in practical mechanics was the repairing of a corn-mill in his native village; after which, before he was eighteen years old, he erected two or three other mills. Determined, however, not to suffer these manual occupations to prevent his pursuing his studies further, he took occasion sometimes to visit Edinburgh, where he attended the courses of lectures on mechanical philosophy and chemistry, by Professors Robison and Black. With the former of these gentlemen he contracted a friendship which had important results on his future course, since, from the professor he received letters of introduction to Messrs. Bolton and Watt, then established at Soho, near Birmingham. Conscious of his powers, the young man now desired a wider sphere for the exercise of his talents than could be found in his own country, and, accordingly, leaving Scotland, he set out for London. On his way, he visited Liverpool, Manchester, and other towns, for the purpose of examining the different mills and public works in those great commercial emporiums. Thence he proceeded to Birmingham, where he spent some months with Messrs. Bolton and Watt, and constructed there several machines which gave proof of his ability. His new friends would willingly have retained him at Soho, but he persisted in his purpose to repair, in the first instance, to London. During his progress he again made a tour through the manufacturing districts of Leeds, Sheffield, and Newcastle. Soon after his settlement in London, he was engaged by Messrs. Bolton and Watt to superintend the works of the Albion Mills. Mr. Watt afterwards gave this testimony to the skill of the young artisan :—"In the construction of the mill-work and machinery, most valuable assistance was derived from that able mechanician and engineer Mr. J. Rennie, then just entering into business, who assisted in placing them, and under whose directions they were executed." He adds that the machinery which used to be made of wood was here made of cast-iron, in improved forms; and he thinks that this was the commencement of that system of mill-work which has been so beneficial in this country.

His biographer in the "Encyclopædia Britannica," adds :—"In fact, Rennie's mills are the most perfect specimens of mechanism in that way that exist, distinguished by a precision of movement, and a harmony and proportion of parts that now serve as models throughout the empire." This undertaking seems to have first led Mr. Rennie to the study of that branch of civil engineering connected with hydraulics, in which he subsequently obtained such high celebrity. It also at once secured for him such reputation in the particular department of mill-work, that he found himself soon in a very extensive line of business. He was applied to by the planters of Jamaica and the other West India islands for their sugar-mills, which he constructed in so satisfactory a manner as to obtain almost a monopoly of those expensive works.

To give an enumeration of all his great productions is beyond the object of this sketch. There are three which will, above all the rest, immortalize his name. The principal, already mentioned, is the Waterloo bridge, the cost of which was more than a million sterling. In a great public work of this description, durability is a primary consideration, and the material employed in this bridge is granite—the most costly and enduring species of building-stone. The piers also were built in coffer-dams. "That a fabric so immense, presenting a straight horizontal line, stretching over nine large arches, should not have altered more than a few inches—(not five in any one part)—from the straight line, is an instance of firmness and solidity utterly unknown, and almost incredible." It cannot be doubted that to Mr. Rennie's skilful distribution of the pressures, and the just proportions which he gave to the several parts, these results are owing. It was always a rule with our architect to make nothing slight; nor would he engage in an undertaking where his requirements as to funds could not be fully met.

His works were all constructed for posterity. It must be added here, that of the five bridges which connect the two banks of the Thames, three have been built from the designs of one man—a fact, as has been well observed, which must throw a lustre on the name of Rennie, and be regarded with feelings of pride by the most distant connection of his family.

The great Canova, when he visited England, and first beheld Waterloo Bridge, said it alone was worth a journey from Rome to see.

As a bold and ingenious piece of mechanism, which may be considered as distinct from positive architecture, there is nothing (says the writer in "Rees' Encyclopædia") in Europe that can bear a comparison with the Southwark bridge. The three immense arches consist entirely of masses of cast-iron, of various forms and dimensions, put together on the same principle as a similar fabric of hewn stone—a method of employing iron which may be considered to form a new epoch in the history of bridge-building. It was apprehended by many that this light and beautiful fabric would suffer materially from the variations of the temperature; but it has stood the test of many winters and summers without appearing to feel either. Mr. Rennie himself, in a letter to M. Ponce on this subject, says: "It is a great pleasure to me to tell you that all the parts of this work have fully answered my expectations; I have not at present discovered any alteration from its original form, nor the least fracture in any of the pieces which compose it. My son, who had noted with scrupulous attention the effects of the expansion and contraction caused by the heat and the cold, purposes publishing one day the result of his observations."

The Breakwater in Plymouth Sound is the third splendid achievement of Mr. Rennie's genius we shall notice. "It can scarcely be called an architectural work, but is constructed on true hydrodynamical principles, and so gigantic in its dimensions and cyclopean in its structure, as to defy equally the force of the waves and the ravages of time."

As a civil engineer, Mr. Rennie before long established his reputation by the survey and execution of the Crinal and Lancaster Canals, and his talents in this department were speedily called into full play, "the rage for canals," at that time pervading every part of the kingdom, giving ample scope for his energies. In fact, the surveys he was called to make were so numerous, that, in a few years, he knew the surface of England, as it were, by heart, and could tell immediately when a canal was projected, what course it should take.

The resources of his mind were also displayed, in all their vigour, in the plans and construction of those magnificent docks which are such an ornament to the metropolis, and of the utmost utility to commerce and navigation. The London Docks, and the East and West India Docks at Blackwall, were executed from his plans and under his direction.

After mentioning several of the principal undertakings in which Mr. Rennie was engaged during the last thirty years of his life, and which, on a rough estimate collected from his reports, did not fall short of forty millions sterling (about twenty of which were expended under his own immediate supervision), his biographer adds,—"Indeed, few great works were carried on, either by the public or individuals, on which he was not either employed or consulted. His industry was very extraordinary. Fond of the society of his select friends, and of rational conversation, he never suffered amusement of any kind to interfere with his business, which seldom engaged him less than twelve hours, and frequently fifteen, in the day. His conversation was always amusing and instructive. He possessed a rich fund of anecdote, and, like his old friend James Watt, told a Scotch story admirably.

As a travelling-companion he was highly entertaining. He knew everybody on the road, and everybody knew John Rennie. Of an ardent and anxious mind, and naturally impetuous, he was gifted with the most perfect self-control, and the irritation of the moment was seen but as a light summer's cloud passing across his finely-marked features, which were on so large a scale, though blended with much mildness as well as dignity, as to obtain for his noble bust by Chantrey, when exhibited in Somerset House, the name of "*Jupiter Tonans.*"

After instituting a comparison between Rennie and Mr. Ramsden, the writer, thus concludes: "They were both equally clear in their mode of communicating information to others, and it is sufficiently remarkable that, in their illustrations, both of them had rarely recourse to any other instrument than a two-foot rule, which each always carried in his pocket. Many a time has the writer derived instruction from the two-foot rules of John Rennie and Jesse Ramsden. They were both equally communicative when they saw that information was desired; and nothing like professional jealousy or selfish feelings actuated either of these ingenious men, who, on the contrary, were always kind and condescending to the more humble artists of their respective professions."

Mr. Rennie married in 1789, and had six children, of whom the two eldest, Messrs. George and John (now Sir John) Rennie, successfully followed the profession of their eminent father, who survived his wife, and, till within a few years of his death, enjoyed excellent health. He died October 16, 1821, and was buried in St. Paul's Cathedral, close to the grave of Sir Christopher Wren.

JACQUES ROUBO,

CARPENTER AND BUILDER.

Born 1739—*Died* 1791.

CARPENTRY is the well-known art of employing timber in the construction of edifices. It is of most general and most important use, and of the highest antiquity, and possesses much interest in relation to the fine arts. It is divided into two branches — carpentry and joinery. The first includes the larger and rougher kind of work, which has to do with the construction and stability of an edifice; joinery (called by the French *menuiserie*, from the *menus bois*, or small woods employed in that art) includes all the interior finishing and ornamental woodwork. To excellence in either of these arts a knowledge of geometry is requisite; and hence the celebrated geometrician Monge thought it necessary to describe the art of carpentry in his "Treatise of Descriptive Geometry," and said that if circumstances had made it desirable for him to devote himself to any trade, he would have chosen that of a carpenter.

This art has made great advances in modern times: and there are numerous admirable examples of construction by various skilful artisans. In accuracy of execution and celerity and minuteness of finish, our workmen are unsurpassed. Some also of the French have greatly excelled in works of ingenious carpentry, among whom is Philibert De Lorme, a celebrated architect in the time of Henry II., who was specially renowned for his method of constructing wooden domes. He invented a new plan of building, which consists in substituting for large pieces of timber deal boards, placed horizontally, in roofs of all dimensions. This idea he first carried out in the erection of the Chateau de la Muette.

The celebrated cupola of the Halle aux Blés at Paris, unhappily consumed by fire in 1802, was built upon this method, which possesses great advantages, especially in lightness of construction and economy of wood; for in this manner a very large roof may be raised with small logs.

This cupola was a masterpiece of art. "It was ornamented by twenty-five rays of panes of glass, producing a fine effect. The eye beheld with astonishment this immense vault of 198 feet in height, 377 in circumference, and 100 feet from the floor of the pavement to its summit. It was impossible to conceive how the dome was sustained, divided thus between wood and glass, and apparently less than one foot in thickness."

Of the origin and construction of this work we have an account given by M. Boileau. The grain-trade had for a long time been confined to the circular galleries of the building, whilst the central open space remained unemployed. At the time of the *fêtes* given in honour of the birth of the Dauphin, son of

Louis XIV., this space was covered by an immense awning, presenting by the light of the illumination a beautiful appearance, which made a strong impression on the imagination of two young architects, Legrand and Molinos, who had then recently returned from Rome. The subject was brought under discussion, and the project conceived of substituting for the awning a permanent roof of wood. But how to effect this? By general consent the difficulties were formidable, for "the roof must not be too heavy for the old foundations." How was it possible to find a builder capable of executing so difficult a task? Some one present at the deliberation of the authorities expressed his opinion that there was but one person in Paris able successfully to undertake such a project. This was Roubo, author of a skilful treatise on the art of building. The result was that a deputation was sent to M. Roubo, with the request that he would engage to do the work. He delayed giving an answer until the next day, when, after due consideration, he consented to undertake the construction of the cupola, but on the sole condition of freedom to follow out his own plans. This being agreed to, he immediately commenced the work, adopting, as we have said, the plan employed by Philibert De Lorme in building the Chateau de la Muette.

After struggling with difficulties of various kinds, and assisting with his own hands in the preparation of every piece of wood in the cupola, aided by Albourg, a carpenter, and Raguin, worker in iron, who executed the iron lantern on the top, Roubo, at the end of five months' labour so well directed as not to endanger a single life, saw his great work completed on the 31st of January, 1783. We are told that when the supports were taken down, Roubo, full of confidence in the system he had adopted, insisted upon standing under a cornice of the platform, in order to examine the roof closely, and observe if it shook when left to its own resources. No one was willing to share with him what everybody considered a great danger. The props were removed amid the acclamations of the people, and the intrepid Roubo was assured of the complete success of his undertaking. He was borne in triumph on the shoulders of the admiring citizens; the crowd pressing on all sides, to gain a sight of the man to whom they owed a construction so novel and useful.

Roubo on this occasion, as well as on all others, proved himself as disinterested as he was enterprising and skilful; and far from enforcing his claims as the originator of such an admirable work, he would only accept the sum agreed upon as a remuneration for superintending the building of the cupola. Ragein, on one occasion, began praising his own lantern to him: "Say nothing about it," replied Roubo; "had I been in your line, I would have built the whole cupola of iron." This idea was actually carried out twenty-five years later. We have selected Roubo from among so many others who have excelled in the same branch of industry principally because he presents a somewhat singular example (especially in a Frenchman) of an artisan who attained distinction in his own line, and who, satisfied to remain a simple operative, never abandoned his business for a higher department of labour. His success and reputation were the result of long and patient industry. He was born in Paris, in 1739, and was the son of a journeyman builder. At an early age he showed remarkable powers of application, and anxious to raise himself above the disadvantages of his circumstances, he diligently applied to study, although there were many discouragements and hardships in his way. One of his biographers says, that when he first began to work at his father's trade, his poverty was so great, that, while he was engaged during the long winter nights in study, he could not afford to pay for a lamp or candle, and was obliged to pick up pieces of tallow and fat thrown out by the neighbours, and burn them.

Such ardour in the pursuit of his object was sure to overcome all obstacles. The little money he could procure was almost all laid out in the purchase of books and models for drawing; and before long he had acquired some knowledge in mathematics, in mechanics, and in designing.

Happily, he soon attracted the attention of Professor Blondel, a nephew of the celebrated architect of that name, who, devoted to the advancement of science, had opened in Paris a public school of architecture, which, during thirty years, he carried on with unwearying zeal. The importance and utility of these labours were sufficiently proved by the celebrity which several of his pupils attained, and by the great advancement of the art consequent on these efforts. He was not long in discovering the merits of Roubo who found in him a generous friend and supporter After giving him gratuitous lessons for five years, and in various ways encouraging and assisting him, M. Blondel had, indeed, great reason to be proud of his pupil.

Encouraged by the fostering aid he thus enjoyed, Roubo soon proved himself as skilful in the theoretic as in the manual department of the art he had studied. At the age of thirty, he presented, for the approbation of the Academy of Sciences, a treatise he had written on the "Art of Building," of which the commissioners appointed to hold the examinations reported so favourably, that the academy decided it should at once be admitted into the authorized collection of works on arts and sciences. This favour was accompanied by one of a marked distinction. In consideration of the talent he had displayed, Roubo was admitted into the freedom of the society, and the academy, by a special decree, accorded him permission to dispense with the customary requisitions.

The work which had been thus honourably received was preceded by the elements of geometry, simplified for the use of the workmen for whom it was designed. The first part treated of the different woods suitable for joinery, and their preservation, with various details relative to the tools, &c.; in short, the subject generally, in its different branches. Then followed the decorative parts of the art; and, in the third division, carriages, furniture, and cabinet-making were treated of; and, in conclusion, the art of trellis-work, or the joinery of the garden. The numerous engravings in the work were all from drawings made by the author himself.

The reputation which Roubo had thus established did not fail to bring him plenty of business, and naturally obtained for him the preference on occasion of any difficult and important undertaking in his line. Thus, as we have already seen, it was to him the authorities had recourse for the cupola of the Corn-hall—which, unfortunately, no longer exists. Other monuments, however, remain to evince his skill; such as the massive staircase of mahogany in the hotel Marbœuf, the vault over the Halle aux Draps; and, above all, his "Art of Building."

As a man of business, Roubo seems deservedly to have enjoyed the respect and regard of all. Active, enterprising, and diligent, he satisfied and exceeded the expectations of his employers; content with his situation, he desired only to excel in his own department, and his time was divided between business and the cares and duties of his family. Unhappily, the whirlpool of the French revolution now swept with desolating effect over the whole country and the metropolis, agitating the minds of the people, and interrupting all the usual avocations and pursuits of men. Roubo, participating in the general excitement, eagerly entered into the contest, and was nominated a director of the National Guard. In this capacity he went, when suffering under the pressure of severe illness, to assist, with his company, at the *fête* of the confederation, and the fatigues he underwent on that occasion produced an access of his disorder, from which he died early in 1791, at the age of fifty-two.

In him we see a favourable example of the simple workman attaining, by sheer industry and unflinching effort, the information necessary to qualify him for practical superiority in the art to which he had devoted his powers.

ALOIS SENNEFELDER,

THE INVENTOR OF LITHOGRAPHY.

Born 1771—*Died* 1834.

A SIMPLE and circumstantial record of the experiments and difficulties attending the invention of a highly important art cannot fail to be interesting, and such a one has been given us by Sennefelder, who wrote an account of his inventions and discoveries, of which an English translation was published in 1819. The history of this persevering inventor, and the trials he encountered, and the obstacles against which he had to struggle in bringing the art of lithography into successful and profitable operation, affords a remarkable illustration of the power of genius to overcome the most adverse circumstances.

He was born at Prague in 1771, and was the son of a comedian at the Theatre Royal, Munich. When very young he showed an inclination to follow the profession of his father, who refused to yield to this predilection in the boy, and sent him to study the law at Ingolstadt; but he does not seem to have shown any turn for legal pursuits, and indulged his favourite inclination by performing occasionally at private theatres, and employing his leisure hours in dramatic composition. He wrote a comedy, which was published, but does not seem to have made any sensation. At the age of twenty he lost his father, and was compelled, from want of pecuniary resources, to discontinue his studies, and he next attempted again to devote himself to the stage. Finding, however, that the inferior parts only were assigned to him, he resolved to try his fortune a second time as an author, and wrote another play, which did not pay his expenses. While this composition was passing through the press, Sennefelder, annoyed at the extreme slowness of the printers, made himself acquainted with the process of printing, and became desirous of securing the necessary apparatus. Being too poor to gratify this wish, he tried to discover some mode of stereotyping, by which he might be able to print his own works with a very small stock of type. He formed a composition of clay, fine sand, flour, and pulverized charcoal, mixed with a little water and kneaded as stiff as possible, and with this paste he made a mould from a page of types, which became in a quarter of an hour so hard that he could take a very perfect cast from it in melted sealing-wax by means of a hard press. He states that by mixing a little pulverized plaster of Paris with the sealing-wax the stereotype plates thus produced were much harder than the common type metal of lead and antimony. The want of means for carrying on this project led him to abandon it.

He then tried etching on copper, but found difficulties arising from his want of practical knowledge, and still more from the expense of the copper-plates, which be ground and polished after using, to make them available for more than one operation. In order to lessen this difficulty, he used a piece of fine stone for his exercises in writing backwards, and afterwards tried printing from it instead of copper, but in this he was not very successful.

The next step towards his discovery was occasioned by a simple incident which strikingly displays the necessitous circumstances in which Sennefelder then found himself. Not being acquainted with the composition used by engravers for covering their etching-ground in defective places, he had invented a kind of chemical ink for the purpose, consisting of wax, soap, and lamp-black. It chanced one day, just as he had polished a stone plate for etching, his mother came to him, requesting that he would immediately write a bill of his linen, which the washerwoman was waiting to take away. Looking around him for a slip of paper, he found that he had not even a scrap at hand, having used all he had in taking off proof-impressions, and, in addition, that his inkstand was dry. The matter being urgent, he hastily wrote out the list upon the prepared stone with his chemical ink, intending to copy it out at leisure. Not long after, when about to clean off this writing, the idea occurred to him that by the application of aqua-fortis and water he might etch the stone so as to leave the writing in sufficient relief for printing from. The experiment proved completely successful, and as soon as he had perfectly satisfied himself as to the importance and practicability of this new method, he at once set about turning it to account so as to gain a livelihood by it.

Again his indigent circumstances stood in the way of his progress. He knew not how to raise the necessary money for the construction of a press, the purchase of stones, paper, and so on—nor did any better resource present itself than that he should enlist as a private in the artillery, and serve as a substitute for a friend, who promised him a premium of 200 florins, which sum he hoped would procure him the means of carrying on his operations in his leisure hours, until he could succeed in procuring his discharge. With this intention he went to Ingoldstadt with a party of recruits, but his purpose was thwarted on its being discovered that he was not a native of Bavaria, and therefore could not serve without a special license. While at Ingoldstadt, he made various inquiries bearing on the subject of his discovery, which led him to conceive that this new process would be peculiarly well adapted for printing music, and he went so far as to suggest it to a musician of the elector's band named Glaissman, who was then preparing some music for publication. In connection with this individual he published a few works, which sufficiently proved the capabilities of the art; and the elector, Charles Theodore, was so well pleased with the efforts of these ingenious printers, that he sent them a present of 100 florins, and promised them an exclusive privilege for the exercise of their art.

Unhappily, the electoral Academy of Sciences, before

which Sennefelder laid a copy of the first work, with an account of the process, acted in a very different manner. As an illustration of the economy of his invention, he had mentioned the small cost of the press; and we may imagine how grievously he was disappointed when, instead of an honourable mention in the "Transactions" of the society, he received a present of twelve florins, accompanied with an intimation from the president that his memoir had been favourably received, and that since, according to his own statement, the expense of the press did not exceed six florins, it was hoped that a compensation of double that amount would satisfy his expectations.

The hopeful prospect which seemed opening before Sennefelder at this time (about 1796) was clouded by the difficulty of constructing a more efficient press than had been used in the first operations. A rolling press had been tried, but owing to some circumstance which had escaped his observation, he failed in his attempts to make a new one. He afterwards constructed a machine, in which the pressure was obtained by a stone of 300 lb. weight falling from a height of ten feet—a plan which produced good prints, but broke the stones after a few impressions.

Having very narrowly escaped being killed by a falling stone in this press, the indefatigable man saw himself obliged to abandon it, and immediately set about constructing another, on a different principle.

So many failures, and the difficulty of obtaining suitable workmen to employ about the new process after a time brought the concern into discredit, and the partners were disappointed in their hope of obtaining their expected exclusive privilege during the life of the Elector Charles Theodore.

The lithographic printing he had hitherto attempted seems to have been mechanical, as Sennefelder informs us that he discovered chemical printing, or lithography —the beautiful art which has since attained so high a degree of excellence and utility—in 1798. Some of the earliest specimens of the art, as applied to pictorial subjects, were vignettes, which he executed to illustrate a catechism, under the superintendence of the Rev. M. Steiner, director of the royal school establishments. In the following year, Sennefelder obtained an exclusive privilege for Bavaria for fifteen years, and soon established a considerable business, in which he employed his two brothers and two apprentices. The process was no longer kept a secret, and many persons visited the office, among whom was the editor, M. André, of Offenbach. With this gentleman Sennefelder entered into partnership, and after a time made arrangements for obtaining patents and setting up presses in Vienna, London, Paris, and Berlin. While engaged in these projects he visited London, but he did not succeed in his purpose there. He had hoped great results from the application of his invention to cotton-printing; but his prospects were blighted by the suspension of commercial intercourse between England and the Continent, under the rule of Bonaparte. He also suffered from the treachery of a person he employed, who divulged some improvements which he had introduced into calico-printing before a patent was secured for them.

On his return to Munich, where his brothers had continued to prosecute the business, he greatly enlarged his establishment, in connection with Baron Arctin and others This partnership continued some years, during which a great variety of works were executed, some of them for the government, not only in music and ornamental printing, but in art-illustration, as in the "Book of Prayers," by Albert Durer.

Several other lithographic establishments were in successful operation in 1809, when Sennefelder at length obtained an engagement which rewarded him for the toils and vicissitudes of the early period of his career, enabled him to marry, and placed him in comfortable circumstances for the rest of his life. At that time a lithographic office was formed for printing the plans of a new survey of the kingdom, of which a large number were required, and Sennefelder was appointed to the office of inspector of the royal lithographic establishment, with a salary of 1,500 florins per annum, and with permission to carry on his private business as well. The subsequent improvements effected by Sennefelder were attributed by himself to the ease and independence which this honourable engagement afforded him. In earlier days, want of means had crippled his energies, and forced him to lose, in solicitations and struggles to obtain help, the time which more ample resources and proper means would have enabled him to turn to good account. Yet, far from complaining of these adverse circumstances, this worthy man rejoiced in the success which had eventually crowned his meritorious efforts, and thus expressed himself upon the subject :—"I esteem myself happy in seeing during my own lifetime the value of my invention so universally appreciated, and in having myself been able to attain in it a degree of perfection, which in a thousand other instances has not been reached till long after the death of the first inventor."

Sennefelder had early commenced making a collection of specimens to illustrate an account of his new art, but circumstances had impeded its completion, until at length, being urged to publish a work which should perpetuate the memory of the discovery, and set at rest the erroneous reports prevalent on the subject, he complied; and in 1819 published a quarto volume, entitled "A complete Course of Lithography," with a portrait, and twenty plates. The illustrations of various styles—some of which are curious—add to the value of the work, which was very shortly translated both into French and English, the latter translation being published by Messrs. Ackermann. Those who wish to study or practise the art in its full extent will do well to consult this book. It has no pretension to literary merit, but is interesting as an original record of the experiments and difficulties connected with the discovery, and contains much valuable information for the practice of the different branches of

In 1819 the Society for the Encouragement of Arts in London spontaneously voted their gold medal to Sennefelder, as the inventor of lithography.

Since that time we have seen almost every year new improvements in this art, so useful in its application to many branches of industry;—by its means not only are transcripts of writings produced with perfect imitation of the handwriting, and faithful copies of pictures executed at a small price, but in manufactures, for ornamenting pottery, china, and porcelain, it has been much in request, as also for printing goods of all kinds—cottons, leather, wood, varnished metals, &c.

Surely the man who thus, by his own ingenuity and well-directed efforts, originated a branch of industry which maintains at the present time many thousands of families, deserves a place among our Heroes of the Workshop!

Sennefelder died at Munich, October 26, 1834, in his sixty-third year.

GEORGE STEPHENSON.

Born 1781—*Died* 1848.

"I have risen from a lower level than the meanest person here; and all I have been enabled to accomplish in the course of my life has been done by PERSEVERANCE!"

GEORGE STEPHENSON is emphatically THE ENGINEER to whose intelligence and perseverance we owe the introduction of railways into England, and who set the first example, in this country, of works which others have successfully carried into execution throughout the world.

Not only is this great man a surprising example of a labourer raising himself to wealth and eminence without a single advantage, except what he derived from his own genius, but the direction which that genius took has stamped his name upon the most wonderful achievement of our age. It is as the originator of railway locomotion that he founds his highest claim to the gratitude of the world, though his powers were shown on many other subjects.

He was born in the colliery village of Wylam, a few miles from Newcastle-on-Tyne, on the 9th June, 1781. His parents were in the lowest ranks of their occupation, but they were industrious, respectable, and amiable. His father is described as an exceedingly kind-hearted man, who encouraged the robins to feed

George Stephenson P. 150

around his engine-fire, and delighted the boys and girls by his stories of Robinson Crusoe and Sinbad the Sailor. So poor were they, that father, mother, four sons and two daughters, all lived together in a one-roomed cottage, and none of the family were sent to school, which was too expensive a matter for their poor means.

George's first employment, at the age of eight years, was crow-keeping, his wages being *2d.* a day. In the intervals of this employment, he found time for making whistles out of reeds, and other occupations more akin to his genius. His favourite amusement was erecting clay-engines, with the help of a chosen companion. They found the clay for the engines in the adjoining bogs, and the hemlock which grew about supplied them with imaginary steam-pipes. At the age of fourteen he was taken to assist his father as a fireman of the colliery, a promotion he had earnestly desired. From that time, he devoted himself so assiduously and successfully to the study of the engine he was appointed to work, that he soon acquired a practical knowledge of its construction and motions; in fact, "it became a sort of pet to him, and he was never weary of watching it." He was thus gradually attaining the character of a clever and improving workman; what he was set to do he tried to do well and thoroughly, never neglecting small matters, but aiming to be a complete workman, at all points.

At this time he was wholly uneducated. There was, however, a night-school in the village, kept by a poor teacher, and this he determined to attend; by which means, at the age of nineteen, he had learned to read correctly, and "was proud to be able to write his own name." He afterwards began to learn arithmetic, in company with one of his comrades, who soon found himself outstripped, "for George took to figures wonderful." The secret of this success was *perseverance.* He worked out the sums in his by-hours, improving every minute of his spare time by the engine-fire, there solving the sums set for him on his slate by his master; and thus his progress was rapid, and, with a ready heart and mind, he soon became well advanced in arithmetic.

He had inherited his father's love of animals, and, like him, used to tempt the robins to hop and fly about the engine-fire with bread crumbs saved from his dinner. He kept blackbirds, too, and he tamed them so successfully, that they would fly about his cottage, unconfined. But his favourite pet was his dog,—so sagacious that he performed the office of a servant, almost daily carrying his dinner to him at the pit, the tin can containing the meal being suspended from the dog's neck; and thus laden, he walked proudly on his road quite through the village, turning neither to right nor left, heedless of the attacks of other curs.

In the year 1801 Stephenson was appointed "brakesman" of a pit in the neighbourhood, with wages of about £1 a week; and he contrived to increase his earnings by mending and making the shoes of his less dexterous fellow-workmen. One of his choicest productions in this line was a pair of shoes for Fanny Henderson, a young servant-girl in a neighbouring farmhouse, whom, at the age of twenty, he married.

He now furnished a small cottage near Wallsend, and settled down as a regular, steady workman, so habitually sober and industrious, that he was quite a standing example of character to his fellows. Never was he known to be "the worse for drink" in his life; and by the manner in which he spent his spare hours he was surely and silently paving the way to be something more than a mere workman. He set himself to study the principles of mechanics, and to master the laws by which his engine worked; and while sitting in the winter evenings beside his sweet young wife, he was industriously employed in making mechanical experiments or in modelling experimental machines. Among his various speculations he occupied himself a good deal in endeavouring to discover that *ignis fatuus* of experimentalists—perpetual motion.

In the year 1803 his only son, Robert, was born—one of the few examples of a son inheriting the genius as well as the peculiar tastes of his father. The child was, from his earliest years accustomed to the habits of steady industry he saw so diligently observed by those around him, and soon became a great delight to his father, whose evening hours were made happier by his presence. But within a twelvemonth after the birth of her little boy, Mrs. Stephenson died, to the great grief of her husband, who never ceased tenderly to cherish her memory.

At this time troubles multiplied upon him. His father met with a distressing accident, and lost his eyesight; the condition of the working classes was very discouraging, in consequence of high prices and heavy taxation; and he was himself drawn for the militia, and had to pay a large sum to provide a substitute. Almost in despair, he entertained the idea of emigrating to America; "but his poverty prevented him from effecting his purpose, and rooted him to the place where he afterwards worked out his career." An interesting feature in Stephenson's character was the strength of his filial attachment. As soon as he had procured sufficient money from his savings, his first step was to pay off his father's debts; and from that time to the old man's death he entirely supported him. Another admirable trait was the care he took to educate his son. Feeling his own great deficiency in this respect, he determined to give the lad a liberal training. "I was, however, a poor man," he said; "and how do you think I managed? I betook myself to mending my neighbours' clocks and watches at night, after my daily labour was done; and thus I procured the means of educating my son."

The time was at hand when his fortunes were about to take a turn. In 1810, an opportunity was afforded him to turn the practical knowledge he had been so long carefully acquiring to account. An engine had been erected at Killingworth colliery of a very imperfect description. Nobody could make it work until George Stephenson applied his powers to it, and he effectually accomplished the object. Though a mere colliery brakesman he had beaten the engineers of the neighbourhood, and he was forthwith appointed engineman to the Killingworth engine, at good wages.

His skill as an engine doctor was now noised abroad, and he was called on to cure all the old, wheezy, and ineffective pumping-machines in the district. "At this time he lived in a cottage near Westmoor Pit, to which he added several rooms, an oven, and a garden, in which latter he contrived to raise by far the best vegetables in the neighbourhood. In the garden he placed a new sort of "fleycraw," to frighten the birds, which was a subject of great admiration to the neighbourhood. He won the women's gratitude by connecting their cradles with the smoke-jack, and thus making them self-acting. He also attached an alarum to the clock of the watchman, whose duty it was to call him in the morning. In a short time his cottage was a sort of curiosity-shop of models, engines, self-acting cranes, and of perpetual, or what he hoped would become *perpetual* motion machines. He also contrived a lamp to burn under water, with which he used to go into the ponds at night, lamp in hand, and thus attract and catch the fish, which rushed wildly towards the flame. At this time, also, he endeavoured, by a sort of lecture, to give some of his fellow-workmen the fruits of his scientific reading, and his acquirements were matter of the greatest wonder to them.

On one of these occasions, he tried to convince the pitmen that the earth was round, and kept turning round; but his auditors flatly declared the thing to be impossible, as it was clear that "at the bottom-side they must fall off!" "Ah!" said George, "you don't quite understand it yet."

In 1812, the engine-wright having been accidentally killed, Stephenson was appointed to be his successor, at a salary of £100 a year, with the use of a horse. In this new position he had far greater opportunities for improving himself than he had hitherto possessed. The subject of the locomotive-engine began to occupy his attention, and he soon obtained a just conception of its extraordinary powers. His son, for whose education he had made such sacrifices, had proved a most apt scholar, and was now able to give him much assistance, and father and son worked diligently together. The idea of applying steam-power to the propulsion of wheel-carriages, had occupied the attention of many inventors since the time of Watt. Wooden rails had long been in use, and afterwards iron began to be substituted for wood. At length, in 1813, a locomotive was tried on one of the roads, but it was unsuccessful. George Stephenson now resolved to try his hand at the construction of a superior machine, and he gave much time and labour to the object, for his whole thoughts were directed to it; and when all others had abandoned the idea of the locomotive in despair, he continued to entertain the most confident expectation of its eventual success, and even went so far as to say, that it would yet supersede every other tractive power.

His first attempt at constructing a "travelling engine," as he then called it, was in 1813. It was at Killingworth Colliery, and with Lord Ravensworth's money. "Yes," said he, many years afterwards, "Lord Ravensworth and his partners were the first to intrust me with money to make a locomotive engine. That was made thirty-two years ago, and we called it 'My Lord.' I said to my friends that there was no limit to the speed of such an engine, if the works could be made to stand it."

Although a considerable advance on others, this machine was somewhat cumbrous and clumsy, and Stephenson was not content till he had undertaken to make a second, into which he might introduce the improvements he saw necessary. Accordingly, in 1815, he had succeeded in manufacturing a machine superior to all others, and "containing the germ of all that has since been effected."

Some years passed away before any further step was taken in reference to this great achievement; so slowly do men receive and act upon new ideas. During that time, his locomotive-engine was in daily use on the Killingworth railway, without exciting much attention. He had no means of bringing his important invention into public notice. He himself well knew its value, and already anticipated its general adoption; but he was an unlettered man, and could not give utterance to the thoughts he cherished on the subject;

and Killingworth Colliery was remote from London, and unvisited by men of science and intelligence, who might have succeeded in drawing attention to the wonderful machine made by George Stephenson. As it was, no notice was attracted towards it, and the "puffing Billy" went on doing its daily quota of hard work, having long ceased to be an object of curiosity in the neighbourhood.

But a grand epoch in the history of our engineer was now at hand. In the year 1821 Mr. Pease, of Darlington, obtained an Act of Parliament for making a railway from Stockton to Wilton, and Mr. Stephenson, hearing of this project, went over to Darlington and introduced himself to Mr. Pease, who, with ready discernment, soon perceived that this was the man he needed.* In consequence of this interview, Stephenson was directed to make a survey of the line, which he immediately proceeded to do. The first rail was laid in May, 1822; and on the 27th September, 1825, the Stockton and Darlington railway was opened for traffic. It was the earliest public highway of the kind, and the most intense curiosity was naturally felt as to the result. Mr. Stephenson himself drove the first engine. The train consisted of six waggons, loaded with corn and flour, then the passengers' coach,

* He liked the appearance of the man. "There was," he afterwards remarked, "such an honest, sensible look about him, and he seemed so modest and unpretending. He spoke in the strong Northumbrian dialect of his district, and described himself as 'only the engine-wright at Killingworth, that's what he was.'"

with directors and friends, followed by twenty-seven waggons—in all a train of thirty-eight carriages. The signal being given, the train started, and it accomplished the transit in perfect safety—"the arrival at Stockton exciting deep interest and admiration." The success of the undertaking was complete.* With pleasure we learn that Mr. Stephenson, when a prosperous man, did not forget the friend who had taken him by the hand in his early days; and Mr. Pease used to show, with much satisfaction, a handsome gold watch, with this inscription, "Esteem and gratitude: from George Stephenson to Edward Pease."

The next important event in the career of this now rising man was his appointment to survey a railway from Liverpool to Manchester. Every possible obstacle was thrown in the way of this project by the landowners and civil engineers, and almost every one interested. The great difficulty in connection with it was the passage across Chat Moss, a bog about four

* The following lines will serve well to depict this first trip of the wondrous engine:—

"Let Greece not boast her Dædalus,
Nor Araby her horses;
A higher wit invents for us
Machines of swifter courses.

Its iron way athwart the plain,
O'er brooks and rivers steering,
Through mountains piercing, and again
From tunnell'd gorge appearing.

Lo! onwards speeds the flying car,
A steaming, puffing wonder;
How folks do stare and smile, as far
They distance thus the thunder!"

miles broad and more than thirty feet deep. It was pronounced "perfect madness" to entertain the idea of carrying a railroad across this swampy district. But the Liverpool merchants were determined to have the line, and they eventually obtained an Act of Parliament, and Mr. Stephenson "at once made arrangements to commence the works, and to do that which the most distinguished engineers of the day had declared no man in his senses would undertake to do."

The draining of the Moss was indeed a most formidable undertaking. At first the obstacles seemed insurmountable; and for weeks the efforts made to form an embankment were unsuccessful. The question was then brought before the board, whether the work should be abandoned? "We must persevere!" was the intrepid answer of Mr. Stephenson. Determined to persist, he carried on his labours still more vigorously, and in six months after the meeting for discussion was held, a locomotive engine and carriage passed over the very spot, carrying a party of the directors' friends to dine at Liverpool.

The idea that bore him up in the face of so many adverse opinions, was that a ship floated in water, and that the Moss was certainly more capable of supporting such a weight than water was; and he knew that if he could once get the material to float, he must succeed.

The railway between these two vast commercial towns being completed, it was determined to set to work locomotive engines upon it, and a competition ensued to produce the best engine for the purpose.

In this struggle Mr. Stephenson came off conqueror. His engine, "the Rocket," carried away the prize; and from that date the railway system may be said to have been established. A double triumph was thus secured, both of his road and his locomotive. What had been ridiculed as an impossibility was now acknowledged as a fact. This engine showed that "a new power had been born into the world, full of vigorous life and strength, with boundless capability of work;" and it is not, perhaps, too much to say that, in establishing the locomotive system, Stephenson, an unlettered, uneducated man, possessing none of the advantages of scientific culture, opposed by the wealth and intellect of the day, did more to advance the civilization of the world than any individual of his age.

The Liverpool and Manchester line was succeeded by a host of railways on all sides. Projectors of every class hastened into the field, and the iron network was spread over the country. As might have been expected, there were very few important undertakings about which Mr. Stephenson was not consulted. In fact (as he said in 1841) there was hardly a railroad in England which he had not to do with.

This was the busiest period of his life; what with the management of his colliery, his locomotive manufactory, and the various railways of which he was the principal engineer, he had scarcely a moment he could call his own. Happily he possessed a vigorous constitution, and had been trained in a hard school; so that he was enabled to pass through an immense amount of fatigue without injury to his health. Many, many nights he snatched his sleep while travelling in his chaise, and at break of day was hard at work, surveying until dark, and this for weeks in succession.

It is well known what extravagance followed the first outbreak of railway speculation, and what follies, crimes, and losses were connected with that wild mania. The most discreditable trickery was practised; but it is greatly to the honour of the man who more than any other was concerned in the construction and working of railroads, that he unswervingly kept the path of integrity and honour. His engines were thoroughly well made; his roads had none but good materials and good workmanship, and he always protested against jobbery, speculation, and all dishonest proceedings. Having thus, in conjunction with his distinguished son, successfully inaugurated our most important railway systems, George Stephenson retired from the labours and anxieties of public life. He had seen his projects carried out to an extent far beyond his most sanguine anticipations, and he wisely resolved to enjoy the sweets of domestic repose for the remainder of his days. His latter years were spent on an estate in Derbyshire, adjacent to the Midland railway, where, engaged in horticulture and in farming, he took delight in rearing and feeding his rabbits, dogs, and birds, and, in short, cultivated the habits and tastes of a plain country gentleman.

He died on the 12th of August, 1848, at the age of

sixty-seven, leaving behind him the highest character for simplicity and kindness of heart, and absolute freedom from all sordidness of disposition. Averse to ostentation, he steadily refused the offers of rank and title which were made him, feeling they would have been but a shadow, adding no real lustre to his name. For some time previous to his death he had devoted much effort and attention to the education of the young, especially in the colliery works.

His remains were followed to the grave by a large body of his work-people, by whom he was greatly admired and beloved; for they had found him to be a kind and considerate master, ever ready actively to promote all that was calculated to secure their good, and they obeyed him willingly, confiding in his good sense and practical benevolence. The truth was, he had long since learned the art of ruling others, when amid the dangers and difficulties of his early career, he had learned to *rule himself*. His energy and ready tact secured their thorough confidence, and—as strong characters always do—he influenced and quickened those whom he governed. When passing through his own workshops, he would frequently point out to his men how to save labour, and to get through their work skilfully and with ease.

He was the zealous friend of mechanics' institutes, and often addressed them, in homely but entertaining style; cheering young men on by relating his own difficulties, which he had overcome by perseverance.

It is impossible here to dwell on the particular

traits of character displayed in the life of this remarkable man. His whole history is a striking lesson, teaching what energy, perseverance, and enthusiasm in the pursuit of a fixed purpose may effect; and we learn from the success which crowned his efforts, that a man may become the master instead of the slave of the circumstances in which he is placed. While we admire the unerring sagacity displayed throughout all his proceedings, and praise the extraordinary energy and unconquerable determination evinced in every step of his career, we cannot fail to love and admire his pure disinterestedness and high integrity.

Of his humanity and amazing intrepidity, the following is a most striking example. One day, in the year 1814, a workman hurried into Mr. Stephenson's cottage, with the startling intelligence that the deepest main of the colliery was on fire. He immediately hastened to the pit's mouth, whither the women and children were fast rushing, with wildness and terror in their faces. Stephenson at once ordered the men to lower him down the shaft in the corve. There was danger—it might be death—before him; but he must go. As those about the mouth of the pit saw him rapidly pass out of sight, and heard from the depths of the shaft the mingled cries of despair and agony, they gazed on the heroic man with breathless astonishment. He was soon at the bottom, and in the midst of the workmen. Leaping from the corve, on its touching the ground, he called out, "Stand back! Are there six men who have the courage to follow me? If so, come, and we will put the fire out." And so they did, by rapidly throwing up a sort of wall around the flames; the atmospheric air was shut out, and the fire extinguished; the people were saved from death, and the mine was preserved.

It has been impossible, within these narrow limits, even to touch on many deeply interesting parts of Mr. Stephenson's history. We can but desire that all our readers should, if possible, peruse his life, and judge for themselves of the true merits of the man of whom all must think with gratitude for the benefits he has conferred, and with admiration for the triumphs his genius has effected.

VAUCANSON.

AUTOMATA.

Born 1709—*Died* 1782.

AMONG automata (or self-moving machines) are properly reckoned all mechanical engines which go by springs and weights, such as clocks, watches, &c. The term, however, is generally applied to mechanism of another description, in which the ingenuity of machinists has performed such marvels as almost surpass the limits of belief.

Historians have, doubtless, exaggerated in their accounts of the wonders of certain of these artificial machines; yet, what we have seen effected in modern times of this description, tends much to diminish our incredulity. For example, King Theodoric, when writing to one of these skilful constructors, says, "By means of your art, metals emit sounds, birds sing, serpents hiss, and you can give to animals a harmony which they have not received from nature." How near an approach has been made to the accomplishment of all this, we shall perceive while speaking of Jacques Vaucanson and his wonderful automata.

This skilful artisan, when he was yet a boy, showed a surprising turn for mechanical invention. He was born at Grenoble, in the year 1709. Of his father nothing is known; but his mother, who had the care of his education, made him her constant companion, and the boy accompanied her in the visits she paid to her female friends, especially on Sundays and *fête* days. On these occasions little Jack was left to his own resources for amusement, while the good dames conversed together; and it so chanced that, in one house he was occasionally taken to, there was a crack in a partition-wall, which the urchin espying, began to peep through. He found, as he did so, that he could see part of the mechanism of a clock, which hung on the adjoining wall. With curious eyes he watched its movements, of which a portion only was visible to him. It was the first time he had ever thought about the subject; but now his attention was attracted, and he resolved he would make himself master of the whole contrivance and ordering of the clockwork. The next time he went there, he took with him a pencil, and occupied himself in drawing as much as he could see of the springs; and in this manner he succeeded in understanding their plan. At length, all at once, he caught the idea of the escapement movement, and before long he contrived, with some pieces of wood and some rough tools, to make a clock, which kept time pretty correctly. His natural genius had thus discovered itself, and he was thenceforward a mechanician, heart and soul devoted to the study of that which he resolved should be his calling in life.

His childish efforts were employed in constructing a baby-house chapel, for which he made little angels that flapped their wings, and some figures dressed as priests, which moved slowly.

He was still but a youth when, chancing to go to Lyons, he heard that a meeting was about to be held for the discussion of a plan for supplying the whole town with water by means of a hydraulic machine. The idea attracted his attention, and he instantly set to work to construct such a machine, and actually succeeded in his purpose, but timidity prevented him from presenting it for approval. Being at Paris some time after, he was filled with surprise and delight to find that the plan of the machine called there the *Samaritaine* was precisely the same as that he had invented at Lyons. This convinced him of his powers, and inspired him with the courage in which he was naturally deficient. He now gave himself up with great diligence to the study of anatomy, music, and mechanics, and for some years occupied himself in this manner.

The flute-player of the Tuileries gave him the idea of constructing a similar work; but he was prevented from undertaking it in consequence of the reproaches of his uncle, who thought it a waste of time; and it was not accomplished until, being laid aside by a long illness, he employed the weary hours of his convalescence in that manner. He succeeded to admiration, and made a small figure, which played the flute with astonishing precision. Some time after he exhibited a tambourine-player; two geese, which dabbled on the ground, looked for corn, and picking it out of a trough, swallowed it. Vaucanson also discovered a means of imitating the animal digestion in a remarkable manner.

In 1740 the King of Prussia, who endeavoured to attach remarkable men to his court, made offers to Vaucanson, who, however, preferred remaining in his own country.

Not long after, Cardinal Fleury engaged his services, intrusting to him the inspection of silk manufactures. He had now a field for the useful employment of his great skill in mechanics in this situation, which he had not sought, but which he owed entirely to the superiority of his talents, perfected by self-culture and long persevering study. His efforts in this department were crowned with success. He brought to perfection an improved method of preparing silk, and constructed various machines, remarkable for the uniformity and precision of their movements, and the consequent regularity of their operation. Of this machinery he gave, in the Record of the Academy of Sciences, of which he was a member, ample and excellent accounts. He possessed in a very rare degree the talent of describing machinery with clearness and precision. He had the gift of perspicacity, and could see with a glance, and describe with equal readiness.

So much importance was attached to these labours, that the jealousy of the ignorant operatives was awakened; and on one occasion, during a journey to Lyons, Vaucanson was pursued and pelted with stones by an angry mob, who threatened to kill him for diminishing the value of their work by means of his machinery. He took a curious mode of revenging himself, in constructing a machine with which an ass executed a piece of flowered stuff!

Another of his remarkable productions was an asp which he made for the representation of Marmontel's Cleopatra. It imitated all the movements of the living reptile, and hissed to the life. This gave rise to a *bon-mot:* some one, being asked his opinion of the merits of the tragedy, replied, "I am of the opinion of the asp!" Vaucanson also made a mechanism to imitate the circulation of the blood, in which Louis XV. took much interest; but he abandoned it, on account of the extreme slowness of the progress made by the royal workmen. Probably he was anxious to confine his attention to more profitable matters.

He had now justly obtained for himself great renown; and the celebrated Voltaire, sharing in the general feelings of admiration entertained for this really remarkable man, wrote some lines in his honour, in which he was compared to Prometheus, who snatched fire from heaven to animate the work of his hands.

In the latter years of Vaucanson's life, he was severely afflicted by long and painful disease; nevertheless, he preserved all his energy and spirit unimpaired. To the very last he employed himself diligently about the construction of a machine he had invented for making an interminable chain—"Lose no time," he cried to his workmen; "perhaps I shall not live long enough to explain perfectly all my idea."

He expired in November, 1782. His valuable collection of machines at the Hôtel de Montagne, he bequeathed to the sovereign. It was at first proposed that this gift should be presented to the Academy of Sciences; but other claims were urged, disputes and difficulties arose, and the result was that the collection was dispersed.

We cannot help regretting that the great skill displayed by Vaucanson was not more usefully directed; for, however curious and ingenious the construction of such works as his automata, this species of labour turns to no serious account, and will never suffice to perpetuate a man's name in the grateful remembrance of his species; whereas, on the other hand, the inventor of a safety-lamp, or of a Jacquard-loom, will never be forgotten.

THE STEAM-ENGINE.

THE MARQUIS OF WORCESTER—SOLOMON DE CAUS—NEWCOMEN—WATT.

" Whirled by the steam's impetuous breath,
  I mark'd yon engine's mighty wheel—
How fast it forged the arms of death,
  And moulded adamantine steel!

But soon—that lifelike scene to stop,—
  The steam's impetuous breath to chill,
It needed but one single drop
  Of water cold, and all was still!"

"The engine of Watt has proved the very Hercules of modern mythology, the united steam-power of Great Britain being equal, it is estimated, to the manual labour of upwards of 400 millions of men, or more than double the number of males supposed to inhabit the globe."—QUARTERLY REVIEW.

How startling are such statistics! It is scarcely possible to overrate the value of an invention by which distance is annihilated, trade rendered prosperous, and human labour saved, and which, within the course of a century, has wholly changed the condition of the mechanical arts in both worlds. To trace the progress of the discovery which, at the present day, works such marvels, is both a curious and interesting task.

There lived, in the time of the emperor Justinian, an architect and engineer named Anthemius, mention of whom is made by Agathius, in the third book of his history. This man having lost a lawsuit, which he had instituted against one of his neighbours, called Tenon, conceived a most singular species of revenge. He filled several large vessels with water, and closed them very tight; several pipes were attached to the covers, which decreased in size as they reached upwards. Fire being placed underneath, the steam escaped through the pipes in the covers; and not finding a free vent above, shook the ceiling and the rafters of his own house, and that of Tenon, to such a degree, that the latter left it, from fright.

The power of steam was clearly known at that early period, but the application of it, for want of means, was never directed to useful purposes. We read, however, in an article by M. Arago, in the "Annuaire des Bureaux des Longitudes" for the year 1829, that 120 years before Christ, Hero, of Alexandria, called "the Old," invented an apparatus presenting the first application ever made of steam. It bore the name of *spiritalia, seu pneumatica,* and is called a reaction-machine.

It was reserved to recent times to conceive the project of making use of steam as a motive power on an extended scale. The idea was first published in England, by the Marquis of Worcester, in a remarkable volume, entitled "A Century of Inventions." He there says:—"This admirable method which I propose for driving up water by fire, possesses illimitable power, if the vessel be strong enough; for I have taken a cannon, which I sealed hermetically, after having filled the interior three-quarters full of water, and then submitted it to the action of fire for twenty-four hours, at the end of which time it blew up with a violent explosion. I subsequently obtained a constant jet of water more than 40 ft. high."

We are assured that the Marquis was indebted for this idea to an unhappy man of genius whom he found incarcerated in the Bicêtre at Paris. This man was a distinguished engineer and architect, born in Normandy, about the close of the sixteenth century. He was for some time in England, where he was attached to the service of the Prince of Wales, and published a work on Perspective; afterwards he went into Germany, and was engaged as engineer by the Elector of Bavaria, who intrusted him with the management of his buildings and gardens. At length he went to France, where he was desirous of obtaining the patronage of Cardinal Richelieu.

We have a glimpse of Solomon de Caus (for that was his name) in the following letter, which was addressed by a lady to Cinq Mars, the celebrated conspirator, who suffered death for his futile attempt to overthrow the power of the great Cardinal Minister:—

"MY DEAR D'EFFIAT,—Whilst you are forgetting me at Marbonne, absorbed in the pleasures of the court and of opposing M. le Cardinal, I, according to your expressed wishes, am doing the honours of Paris to your English lord, the Marquis of Worcester. I take him about, or rather he takes me about, from one curiosity to another. Choosing always the most sad and serious words, speaking but little, listening with great attention, and fixing his large blue eyes upon every one of whom he asks a question, as if he could see into the depths of their souls, he is never satisfied with the explanations he receives, and does not look upon things exactly as they are shown to him. For instance, when we visited the Bicêtre, he pretended to see marks of great genius in a crazy man, whom, if he were not raving, I am sure your Englishman would have taken to London, if possible, and listened to his nonsense from morning till night. As we crossed the yard filled with these creatures, I was half dead with fright, and leaned against my companion. Suddenly an ugly face appeared behind the bars, and a hoarse voice exclaimed, 'I am not crazy. I have made a discovery which will enrich the country that so violently opposes it.' 'What is his discovery?' I asked the man who showed us over the place. 'Ah!' exclaimed he, shrugging his shoulders, 'something very simple, which you would never guess;—it is the use of steam.' I burst out laughing.

"'His name,' continued the keeper, 'is Solomon de Caus. He came from Normandy, four years ago, to present a memoir to the king on the subject of the marvellous effects to be obtained by his invention. According to him, machinery could be moved by it, carriages propelled, and numerous other wonders effected. . . . The Cardinal sent away the fool without listening to him. But De Caus, undiscouraged, followed him from place to place, until Richelieu, weary of his importunities, had him shut up in this place, where he has now been three years and a half. He tells every stranger he sees, as he tells you, that he is not crazy, but has made a grand discovery. He has even written a book upon the subject.' And so saying, he handed us a book. My Lord Worcester took it, and, after reading some pages, said, 'This man seems by no means insane; and were he in my country, instead of being shut up, he would have made his fortune. Bring him hither. I wish to question him.' He returned from this conversation with a sorrowful countenance. 'Alas! he is indeed crazy now,' said he; 'misfortune and captivity have for ever destroyed his reason; this cruel usage has made him mad. But, when you put him in this prison, you incarcerated the greatest genius of his day.'

"Hereupon we took our leave, and since then he has done nothing but talk of Solomon de Caus. Adieu, my dear Henry; come back soon, and meantime forget not—MARION DELORME."

The book shown by the keeper to the Marquis of Worcester was, in all probability, that published by this unfortunate De Caus at Frankfort, in 1615, entitled, "Raisons des Forces Motives," &c. (Considerations of Motive Forces).

Brancas, a philosopher of Rome, was the first who employed the force of steam to produce motion. He contrived a number of different kinds of mills, to be worked by the steam coming from a large æolipile and blowing against the floats or vanes of a wheel. This ingenious invention, with several others, he published at Rome, in 1628, in a work called "La Machine," in which was given a representation of his "fire-engine." But the force he could thus have obtained from the vapour would have been found altogether inconsiderable if he had ever put it in practice.

Thirty years after the publication of the Marquis of Worcester's "Century of Inventions," his discovery was reproduced, almost simultaneously, by an Englishman, named Captain Thomas Savery, and a French physician, named Papin; but the former alone turned it to practical use, and in the year 1698 obtained a patent for a new invention "for raising water and occasioning motion to all sorts of mill-work, by the impellant force of fire." This engine displayed much ingenuity, and was almost as perfect in its contrivance as the same kind of engine has been made ever since that time. It made much noise, and became a general subject of conversation with the engineers and mechanics in the neighbourhood, among whom was one Thomas Newcomen, an ironmonger of Dartmouth, in Devonshire, who was in the habit of visiting the mines of tin and copper in Cornwall, where Captain Savery was well known, from his attempts to introduce his engine for the draining of mines, which, at that period, were nearly all of them at a stand, for want of some more powerful and cheap machines than hand-pumps or horse-machines.

To Newcomen we owe the application of a piston with machinery, by which the action of the atmosphere upon the piston is made to operate, with safety and effect, against the most severe pressures. It would seem Savery claimed for himself the whole merit of the discovery; but posterity has assigned the palm of honour to the modest discoverer of the principle of condensation; for this invention has always been known as "Newcomen's, or, the Atmospheric Steam-Engine."

To Mr. JAMES WATT is due the honour of perfecting, or one might almost say reinventing, the steam-engine. His name is too celebrated, and his discoveries too well known, to need more than a general reference to them here. He was born in 1736, at Greenock, where his father was a merchant and magistrate, and he early showed a marked taste for those pursuits by which he subsequently attained his great and well-earned fame. His grandfather and uncle were both teachers of the mathematics, and the boy's natural turn for mechanics was fostered by those around him. It is related of him, that a friend of his father's one day found the child stretched on the floor, drawing with chalk numerous lines that intersected each other. He advised sending the young idler, as he thought him, to school; but his father bade him first examine what the little fellow was about. On doing so, they found he was trying, at six years old, to solve a problem in geometry. He soon constructed a small electrical machine and other things; and a curious anecdote, related by one of his family, seems to show that already the boy's mind was directed with curiosity towards the marvellous attributes of steam. His aunt, Mrs. Muirhead, not sharing in the general opinion of her nephew's superior abilities, rebuked him one evening for his listless idleness. He would do nothing, she said, but take off the lid of the kettle and put it on again, holding sometimes a cup and sometimes a silver spoon over the steam, watching the vapour as it came out of the spout, and counting the drops of water into which it became condensed!

Chemistry was a favourite subject with him when he was confined by ill-health to his father's dwelling; and, though his naturally feeble constitution prevented him from benefiting much by school instruction, the ardour of his mind was unquenchable, and he devoured every kind of learning.

At the age of sixteen the young philosopher was articled as an apprentice, to learn the business of "an instrument-maker," which included "the making and repairing of the instruments used in mechanics and natural philosophy, and the manufacture, in a rough way, of all kinds of musical instruments, and all the various instruments necessary for the practice of land-surveying."

It was while in Glasgow, on a visit to one of his aunts, that he became interested in the operations of the individual to whom he was apprenticed,—a mechanic who is described as "eking out a scanty subsistence by making and repairing fishing-tackle, and the simple instruments used in mechanical drawing." He was, we are told, "a useful man at almost everything"—just the very man after Watt's own heart, and from whom he learned the rudiments of instrument-making, and, probably, many other useful things which he afterwards turned to account.

After about a year spent in this kind of apprenticeship, Watt went to London, desirous to obtain better instruction in an art then little practised in Scotland. For this purpose he placed himself with a mathematical and nautical instrument maker, under whom he acquired ready and orderly methods of despatching business; but, by sitting too near the door of the workshop in winter, he caught a severe cold, the effects of which he continued to feel to an advanced period of life. In consequence of this illness he was soon compelled to return to Glasgow, where he intended to establish himself in business; but not being a burgess, he was looked upon by the corporations of arts and trades as an intruder upon their privileges, and they refused to allow him to set up even the humblest workshop.

The University of Glasgow came to his assistance at this juncture, and gave him permission to establish himself within their precincts, and also honoured him with the appointment of their mathematical instrument maker. This happened about 1757, when he had scarcely attained his twenty-first year. He was now placed in a congenial sphere, and in the course of a few years was employed and befriended by men of great names, his reputation daily increasing as a diligent and successful cultivator of science. In his profession he showed much ingenuity and skill, and his superior intelligence soon enabled him to form habits of intimacy with the first-rate men of talent at that time in Glasgow. His workshop became a favourite resort of all zealous students and enlightened inquirers into physical science, and was particularly frequented by the pupils of the University. One of these young men (afterwards Professor Robison) expressed the surprise he felt when, on being introduced to Watt, whom he expected to find merely an intelligent workman, he found a philosopher as young as himself, yet willing and able to instruct him or any of the students who might fall into difficulties. In fact, he needed but a sufficient spur to take up and conquer any subject. Without neglecting his business in the daytime, he devoted his nights to various and often profound studies; and however great the difficulties of a subject, provided it were worthy of pursuit, he would follow it out with all the energy of his indefatigable character.

His attention was first specially directed to the subject of the steam-engine in 1763, when he undertook to repair a working model of Newcomen's engine, belonging to the University. During the course of this employment he perceived great deficiencies in the machine itself, which he set himself to remedy, and in the course of his numerous experiments he effected such marvellous results as produced an entire revolution in the working of these machines, the operation of which was speedily felt in every branch of manufacturing industry, and gave a new impulse to universal trade. Professor Robison has given some interesting details with reference to this subject. He says the model was at first a plaything to Mr. Watt and himself (who was at that time a constant visitor to his workshop), but, like everything else which came into the hands of this acute observer, it soon became a most serious study. Being an exact copy of a real engine, it offered a fair opportunity for experiments, and Mr. Watt made many very curious ones. He early perceived that an enormous quantity of steam was wasted, and that the chief improvements the engine was susceptible of must consist in contrivances for increasing its production and diminishing its waste. Professor Robison feeling his mind "fired with the inexhaustible fund of instruction and entertainment" which he beheld opening before him, assiduously attended to the investigations carried on by Mr. Watt, and marked with deep interest his progress. He has given a graphic and amusing sketch of what passed on one occasion :—"About a fortnight after this (in 1765) I came to town, and went to have a chat with Mr. Watt, and to communicate to him some observations I had made. I came into his parlour without ceremony, and found him sitting before the fire, having, lying upon his knee, a little tin cistern, which he was looking at. I entered into conversation on what we had been speaking of at our last meeting—something about steam. All the while, Mr. Watt kept looking at the fire, and laid down the cistern at the foot of his chair. At last he looked at me, and said briskly, 'You need not *fash* yourself any more about that, man; I have now made an engine that shall not waste a particle of steam. It shall all be boiling hot,—ay, and hot water injected, if I please.' So saying, Mr. Watt looked with complacency at the little thing at his feet, and seeing that I observed him, he shoved it away under a table with his foot. I put a question to him about the nature of his contrivance; he answered me rather drily. I did not press him to a further explanation at that time, knowing that I had offended him a few days before, by blabbing a pretty contrivance which he had hit on for turning the cocks of the engine."

The next day Professor Robison met Mr. A. Brown, a very intimate acquaintance of Mr. Watt's, who immediately said, "Well, have you seen Jamie Watt yet? He'll be in high spirits now with his engine, isn't he?" "Yes," said I, "very fine spirits!" "Gad," says Mr. Brown, "the condenser is the thing; keep it but cold enough, and you may have a perfect vacuum, whatever be the heat of the cylinder!" The instant he heard this, the Professor says the whole flashed on his mind at once, and he felt no doubt that Watt had invented a perfect machine.

Some months later he again saw Mr. Watt, who frankly told him all his contrivance, informed him of many curious properties of steam, relative to its heat and elasticity; explained his methods of condensation, and mentioned a number of remarkable facts relative to this subject.

Long afterwards Professor Robison discovered that the little apparatus he had seen on his friend's knee, and which he had shoved under the table with his foot, was the condenser, in his first experiment. "I can say with great confidence," he adds, "that nothing ever occurred to Mr. Watt, either by reading or information, of his leading principle of a steam-vessel perpetually and universally hot. All the other contrivances, of separate condenser, air and water-pumps, amalgam, or rosins, or fats, for keeping the piston air-tight, are but so many emanations from this first thought; and I must say further, that the thought was all his own."

In the summer of 1764 Mr. Watt married his cousin, Miss Miller, and, leaving the college, took up his abode in the town, and opened a shop in the Salt Market, where his increasing business made him soon require the labours of an assistant. During the whole of his residence in Glasgow he practised housekeeping on a very humble scale; but his home was rendered happy by the presence of an excellent woman whom he tenderly loved. Her influence was always exerted to cheer and animate her husband, whose powerful mind was often overshadowed with gloom under the depressing circumstances of indifferent health (for he suffered from the pressure of long-continued nervous headaches), narrow means, and spirits prone to

despond. She ever encouraged his hopes, and when for a time these seemed to be quite overthrown, her buoyant spirits did not sink, nor did her cheerful faith fail; but with true fortitude she went hoping on, and wrote to him, "Do not make yourself unhappy, though things should not succeed to your wish. *If it* (the new steam-engine) *will not do, something else will.* Never despair."

The success of his first experiments on the engine had induced him to determine on constructing a larger model than could be conveniently made at his usual place of business, and he therefore set up this machine, with the aid of his ingenious apprentice, in one of the rooms of a pottery which he had assisted in establishing near Glasgow. An accident put an end to his experiments with this engine; and for want of leisure and means, his project was, at the time, laid aside.

In addition to his employment as a mathematical instrument maker, Watt devoted now much of his time to land-surveying, and this led to the employment of his superior talents in the more important department of civil engineering. In his surveys he used an improved micrometer, and a machine for drawing in perspective, both which he had himself invented.

In the year 1773, having lost his admirable wife, he was induced to settle in England, and enter into partnership with the well-known Mr. Boulton, of Birmingham, a man of wealth, position, and energy, eminently qualified to bring into practical operation the great invention of the improved steam-engine. Nothing could have been more happy than this connection, which lasted more than a quarter of a century, and issued in the successful completion of the arduous undertaking. Assisted by the expert artisans now placed at his command, Watt completed, by the latter end of 1774, his fourth model engine, which, after careful examination, was deemed highly satisfactory. Yet the patentees well knew that much still remained to be done before it could be brought into extensive operation; that costly machinery must be constructed, to aid in the production of new engines; and that a protracted struggle with ignorance and prejudice must be expected before any remuneration could be hoped for. Of the spirited manner in which the mercantile part of the affair was conducted, some idea may be formed from the fact that more than £47,000 were spent before any profits were realized; but at length they began to pour in, and in no scanty measure.

Of the private character of this extraordinary man, a most pleasing account is given by Lord Jeffrey, who observes that perhaps no individual in his age possessed so much and such varied information; he had read so much, and remembered what he had read so accurately and well. His stores of general knowledge were immense, and still more astonishing was the command he always had over them. It seemed as if every subject casually started in conversation was that which he was best acquainted with. In social discourse he made everything so clear, plain, and intelligible, that all were instructed and pleased; and being of a generous and affectionate disposition, he was always ready to impart information, and to assist and encourage those who applied to him for advice or help. An interesting picture is drawn of his personal appearance and manner, by a lady* who knew him when she was a child, and who thus describes the impression he made in society :—" His eye and countenance were calm, as if patiently investigating or quietly contemplating his object. His utterance was slow and unimpassioned, deep and low in tone, with a broad Scottish accent ; his manners gentle, modest, and unassuming. In a company where he was not known, unless spoken to, he might have tranquilly passed the whole time in pursuing his own meditations. But this could not well happen ; for, in point of fact, everybody practically knew the infinite variety of his talents and stores of knowledge. When Mr. Watt entered a room, men of science, men of letters, nay, military men, artists, ladies, even little children, thronged round him. I remember a celebrated Swedish artist having been instructed by him that rats' whiskers make the most pliant and elastic painting-brush. Ladies would appeal to him on the best means of devising grates, curing smoky chimneys, warming their houses, and obtaining fast colours. I can speak from experience of his teaching me how to make a dulcimer and improve a Jew's-harp. On one occasion Mr. Watt visited Paris. It so happened that

* Mrs. Schimmelpenninck.

while going through one of the palaces,—I believe the Tuileries,—a French housemaid appeared much perplexed concerning some bright English stoves which had just been received, and which she knew not how to clean. An English gentleman was standing by, to whom she appealed for information. This was the great statesman Charles James Fox; he could give no help. 'But,' said he, 'here is a countryman of mine who will tell you all about it.' This was Mr. Watt, to whom he was at the moment talking, and who accordingly gave full instructions as to the best mode of cleaning a bright grate." This anecdote Mrs. Watt used to tell with great diversion.

This illustrious man, and great public benefactor, attained the advanced age of eighty-four. As his death approached, he was perfectly conscious of his situation, and calm in the prospect of approaching eternity, expressing his thankfulness for the length of days he had been permitted to enjoy, and for the quiet and cheerful evening of life granted him after the prolonged labours of life had terminated.

His useful and honourable course had secured him the admiration of all the great and good men of his day, and when he sank to the grave, the whole nation hastened to pay to his memory the tribute which all acknowledged was his due. "The civilized world,' says his distinguished biographer (Lord Brougham), "is filled with imperishable records of his genius, and the grateful recollection of the whole species embalms his memory." In Westminster Abbey is the noble monument raised to him by the genius of Chantrey—it is his greatest work ;—and the inscription it bears, written by the pen of Lord Brougham, is so beautiful that we transcribe it here :—

"Not to perpetuate a Name
Which must endure while the peaceful arts flourish,
But to shew
That mankind have learned to honour
Who best deserve their gratitude:
The King,
His Ministers, and many of the Nobles
And Commoners of the realm,
Raised this monument to

JAMES WATT;

Who, directing the force of an original genius,
Early exercised in philosophic research,
To the improvement of

THE STEAM-ENGINE,

Enlarged the resources of his country,
Increased the power of Man,
And rose to an eminent place
Among the most illustrious followers of Science
And the real benefactors of the world.

Born at Greenock, 1736.
Died at Heathfield, in Staffordshire, 1819.

Surely such a tribute must make the heart of every Englishman and every philanthropist rejoice!

JOSIAS WEDGWOOD

Born 1730—*Died* 1795.

"They have embodied classical models in a domestic manufacture, like the Wedgwood china."—QUARTERLY REVIEW.

DURING the reign of Queen Elizabeth attempts were made to establish factories of pottery in England; and in the following century a species of enamelled stone-ware was produced in Staffordshire; but little of importance was accomplished till a second Palissy arose in England, in the person of Josias Wedgwood. The career of this remarkable man ranged from 1760 to 1795. Under him the ceramic art in our own country was raised to a high standard of excellence, and from him the admirable productions of more recent periods must be considered to have been derived.

He was the younger son of a Staffordshire potter, and was born on the 12th July, 1730, at Burslem, the principal seat of the potteries. In order fully to appreciate the surprising improvements made by him in this branch of industrial art, it will be necessary to take a glance at the state of the manufacture before his time.

Earthenware is made in several parts of this country, but is so extensively produced in the north-west of

Staffordshire as to have obtained for that district the distinguishing name of "Potteries." This locality extends about ten miles in one direction and two or three in another, and contains some nine or ten towns and hamlets closely contiguous, or actually connected. The aspect of the region is far from ornamental or picturesque in character. "Rows of brick-built houses, interrupted by pottery-works, whose object is indicated by huge cones of bricks, kilns, or baking-ovens, tall chimneys, clouds of smoke, dust in summer and mud in winter, with workmen wearing small closely-fitting skull-caps of drab felt,"—such are the prominent features of the scene. The soil presents almost everywhere a rich variety of clays of various textures and hues, with coal in such abundance that formerly it was to be obtained at one shilling per ton.

To these advantages, joined to the inaptitude of the soil for the purposes of husbandry, is doubtless owing its selection as the site of its present staple manufactures. We are told that some species of earthenware has existed here "for centuries past;" and the fact that many vessels of Roman manufacture, stamped with the Roman name "Attilianus," as well as bricks cemented together, have been found in the neighbourhood, has led to the belief that it was in former ages the site of a pottery. At Burslem, pots to hold butter were made early in the fifteenth century (for which Parliament legislated in the year 1670, requiring the pots to hold just 6 lb. and no more). In the course of time the articles of the manufactory became more various, but the productions were coarse and clumsy, made from clays found in the immediate neighbourhood, painted and moulded in a rude way, and glazed with lead ore finely powdered and sprinkled upon the pieces of ware before firing.

The first improvements in the art must be ascribed to two Dutchmen, the brothers Elers, who came from Holland, and settled at Burslem about the year 1700. They introduced a new kind of glaze, made by casting salt into the kiln when at its greatest heat, which produced a vitrification of the clay on the surface. This was followed by other improvements. A species of red unglazed china was carried by them to such a degree of excellence that some of their teapots sold at a guinea each. They also produced a black variety, obtained by the introduction of manganese into their clays; and their skill in the art is sufficiently attested by the specimens of their labours which still exist.

The next step in advance was the introduction of flint as an element in the composition of the ware itself. It is said this discovery was accidentally made about the year 1720, when a potter named Astbury, being on his way to London, happened to notice the pure white of some burnt flint stone when mixed with water which had been prepared by the ostler of the inn, as a remedy for some disease in his horse's eye. He was struck with the idea that his ware might be improved by an addition of this material, and the experiment succeeded beyond his expectations. Thus originated the white stone-ware, which soon superseded the coloured ones. At first the flints were pulverized, to the terrible injury of the health of the workmen, till the famous Brindley, at an early period of his life, constructed the mills afterwards used for grinding them in a moist state.*

A great improvement was manifest upon the introduction of flint in combination with the clays; and a number of persons engaged in the trade, and largely extended its operations. For a time the art continued to progress, and considerable quantities of the Staffordshire wares found their way into the foreign markets, notwithstanding the increased demands for home consumption. Unhappily, as the potters increased in prosperity they relaxed in care, and, furiously competing with each other in the cheapness of production, inundated the markets with vast quantities of inferior goods. The French speedily took advantage of this state of things; and having succeeded in manufacturing a white ware better glazed and more elegant in form than ours, shipped it in

* A work written in the strange local dialect, and published by a native resident in the district, records this fact in the following manner:—Two old men are sitting together in a publichouse at Burslem, talking over early days, and one says, "Rafy, oi rek'n thee remembers th' oud schemer Brindley, working at th' millu-reet's shop i' th' yard?" His fellow answers, "Ya, that oi doo, varry weel. It wur at th' teyme 'ut he wur bildin the woindy mill i' th' top o' th' Jenkins, for t' groind flint, ur. That's no mych more nor fifty year sin. It wur thout a famous job t' think o' groindin' flint loike fleawr." The "old schemer Brindley" did indeed do "a famous job" for the poor workmen, to whom the dry grinding of flint was so fatal an operation that they are said rarely to have survived the second year of their engagement

large quantities to this country, where it speedily superseded the native productions. Such was the luckless position of the English potters, threatening the speedy overthrow and final ruin of their trade, when the object of this sketch commenced his career.

It may well be believed that but little school learning fell to the lot of the boy, when we are told that "scarcely any person in Burslem learned more than mere reading and writing, until about 1750, when a free-school was endowed, for teaching youth to read the Bible, write a fair hand, and know the primary rules of arithmetic." So low was the social position of the class to which he belonged, and the little opportunity he had for self-improvement is only too evident from the fact that, at the age of eleven years, Josias worked in his elder brother's pottery as a *thrower*, their father being already dead. The small-pox, which left an incurable lameness in his right leg, so as afterwards to necessitate amputation, compelled him to relinquish the potter's wheel. Confined by this affliction for some time within doors, he occupied himself in studying clays and mineral substances, and trying various small experiments in his art.

Nothing is recorded of his further progress till after he had attained the age of twenty-one, when he left Burslem, and connected himself with a man named Harrison, at Stoke (one of the neighbouring villages). During this engagement, which was dissolved at the end of two years, he is said to have first evinced his talent for the invention of ornamental pottery.

He then (in 1754) went into partnership with Mr. J. Whieldon, and manufactured spoons, knife-handles, table and other plates, and various "small crocks;" some of which articles were made in imitation of agate, tortoiseshell, jasper, and porpyhry.

His associate, however, being unwilling to embark in these new branches of invention, for which he had so decided a predilection, he left him at the end of five years, and returned to Burslem, where he first went into business on his own sole account, and set up a pot-work in a small thatched manufactory, upon the spot at present occupied by the new market-house. There he continued to make similar ornamental works, and throve well, at the same time continually experimenting, with a view to further improvements.

His business increasing, he before long took a second manufactory, where he fabricated a white stone-ware; and afterwards a third, at which he produced the cream-coloured ware, which established his reputation in the market, and which was not only handsome in design, but durable, covered with a beautiful glaze, and proof against sudden alternations of heat and cold. Of this exquisite production Wedgwood presented some specimens to Queen Charlotte, who immediately ordered a complete table-service, directing it to be called the "Queen's ware;" and Wedgwood received the appointment of "Potter to the Queen." This illustrious patronage rendered the beautiful novelty so popular, that orders flowed in upon its successful inventor faster than he could execute them.

It should not be forgotten that Wedgwood's success was not the result of any fortunate discovery accidentally made, but that it was due to patient investigation and unremitting efforts. In prosecuting his investigations, he was guided by sound scientific principles, while, with ardent and indefatigable energy, he devoted himself entirely to the object. At the same time, he sought a higher class of workmen than had formerly been employed, to assist him in his labours, and was well seconded by their industrious ingenuity. By varying and repeating his experiments, he succeeded in discovering the mode of manufacturing many other descriptions of earthenware and porcelain, adapted to various purposes of use and ornament. While thus carrying on his improvements, he applied himself to the study of chemistry; and for his further assistance engaged Mr. Chisholme (who had been employed in a similar department by the celebrated Dr. Lewis, author of the "Commercium Philosophico-Technicum"), for whom he not only built a comfortable habitation near the manufactory, but, with generous liberality, when the infirmities of age had disabled him, allowed him an annuity for his support, which was continued till his death.

At the period when Wedgwood commenced his career, the means of intercourse were miserably insufficient. Pottery wares were conveyed in small crates, by pack-horses, or carts, along the wretched roads, while materials for the manufacture travelled after the same fashion. No sooner was the idea of the canal system started than Wedgwood, immediately perceiving its immense advantages, not only to himself but to all engaged in the pottery trade, eagerly co-operated with Brindley, who was then projecting the "Grand Trunk," and actually turned up the first clod of earth for it, in his own neighbourhood. Immediately on the passing of the Act, he bought the land on which the village of Etruria now stands (and which is intersected by the canal), and commenced the erection of his manufactory while the canal was digging. There, in the summer of 1769, he set to work and built a large mansion for himself, at a convenient distance from the works, and suitable dwellings for his workpeople. This is now a neat village, presenting a scene of industrious and profitable labour, the sight of which cannot fail to recall most pleasantly the memory of its celebrated originator.

Finally, leaving Burslem, he removed thither in 1771. About this period, the antique specimens of terra-cotta collected by Sir W. Hamilton at Naples, awakened much interest. They were called Etruscan vases, and exhibited fine specimens of an art the secret of which had been lost for ages. Mr. Wedgwood immediately set about imitating them, and soon, by the aid of encaustic colours of his own composition, produced a series of the most accurate and beautiful copies, which sold at a high price and met with a large demand. It was from this new branch of his art that he called his mansion Etruria, which classical appellation is abbreviated among the population of the district into the familiar-sounding name of "Trury."

In the mean time Mr. Wedgwood had opened a warehouse in London, where the productions of his skill were offered to inspection, and in his partner, Mr. Richard Bentley (son of the Archdeacon Bentley, of Ely), he found a valuable coadjutor, whose extensive knowledge in many departments of literature and science, and acquaintance with many eminent patrons of art, greatly assisted him in the higher branches of his manufacture, and especially in obtaining the loan of specimens of sculpture, vases, cameos, intaglios, medallions, and seals, suitable for imitation by some of the processes he had discovered.

We learn from Dr. Bancroft, that almost all the finely diversified colours which were applied by our artist in his pottery were produced only by the oxides of iron. In the manufacture of the beautiful jasper ware, which rivalled the productions of antiquity, and which found its way into the collections of the curious in all parts of Europe, he employed the native sulphate of barytes, and from this use of it derived great profit, till, by the treachery of a servant, the secret was disclosed and sold, when others employed inferior workmen at a reduced salary, and thus prevented him from employing his exquisite modellers on that branch of the manufacture.

Six other distinct inventions in earthenware and porcelain are ascribed to Wedgwood, besides the Queen's ware, all of which continue to be produced. 1. A terra-cotta, resembling porphyry and granite; 2. The basalt, or black ware, which strikes fire with steel, receives a high polish, serves as a touchstone for metals, resists all acids, and bears the strongest fire without injury; 3. The white biscuit-porcelain, of a smooth, wax-like surface, and of similar properties to the basalt; 4. The jasper ware, so much admired, with its beautiful blue body and pure white raised figures; 5. The bamboo or cane-coloured biscuit porcelain; 6. A porcelain admirably adapted for mortars and other vessels used by chemists.

The most remarkable of all his productions, and the one which has been considered his masterpiece, was his perfect imitation of the Barberini or Portland vase, which was discovered in the tomb of Alexander Severus. On its being offered for sale in London, he wished to purchase it, and bid high against the Duchess of Portland, until, his object being ascertained, he was offered the loan of the treasure for an indefinite period. It was then knocked down to the duchess for the sum of 1,800 guineas. Fifty copies of it were executed, and sold at the price of £50 each; but so great was the expense of its production, that it exceeded the amount thus obtained. Mr. Webber is said to have received 500 guineas merely for modelling it.

The prosperity attained by Mr. Wedgwood at this period of his career was quite unprecedented, both as to the interest excited by his extraordinary talents and the consequent remuneration he obtained; but the results of his skill and energy were far from being confined to his private advantage. They were, in a high degree, valuable to the commercial interests of the country.

In 1785 he was examined before a parliamentary committee, and from the evidence he gave, the inportance of the Staffordshire manufactures to the national interests became apparent. He stated in evidence, that from 15,000 to 20,000 people were then employed in the district called the Potteries, and much greater numbers in digging coals for them, and in preparing flints and clays for the manufacture. He showed the immense amount of inland carriage they created, and the employment they afforded to coasting vessels, even then amounting to 20,000 tons annually. From various other particulars, he illustrated the prosperous state of the manufacture, which he further proved by the statement that, notwithstanding the intolerable duties laid on British ware by foreign states, at least five-sixths of the quantity made were exported. His modesty led him to state that he considered the art of pottery but then in its infancy—a conjecture which has not been verified by subsequent experience.

In the year 1783 he was elected a member of the Royal Society, and in 1786 of the Society of Antiquaries. He carried on an extensive correspondence with the most eminent scientific men, both at home and abroad, and published various pamphlets on the subject of his business, particularly an address to the workmen in the Potteries, dissuading them from entering into the service of foreign manufacturers, which is said to have had the best results. In May, 1782, he addressed to the Royal Society a communication on an instrument he had invented for measuring intense degrees of heat, called a pyrometer. This paper was printed in the 72nd volume of the Society's Transactions. He also planned and carried into execution a turnpike road, ten miles in length, through the Potteries. He was, besides, the founder and one of the principal leaders of the association called "The General Chamber of the Manufacturers of Great Britain."

It is delightful to know that this admirable man was endeared among his intimates by his social virtues and genuine benevolence. The large fortune which he realized by his unwearied labours enabled him to indulge these amiable dispositions; and it is said of him, that he was never known to neglect the claims of any institution he thought likely to promote the good of his fellow-creatures. Especially we rejoice to learn that he consecrated the efforts of his inventive skill to the service of humanity, and rendered them promotive of the cause of freedom and progress. In this connection we may be allowed to notice two cameos of his manufacture,—one of a slave in chains, of which he distributed many hundreds, with a view of exciting the humane to assist in the abolition of the slave-trade; and the other a cameo of Hope, attended by Peace, Art, and Labour, which was made of argillaceous earth brought from Botany Bay, to which place he sent many of them, in order to show what the native materials were capable of, and to encourage the industry of the inhabitants. Such graceful and lovely acts well merit the tribute paid to our great potter in the following lines :—

> "Whether, O Friend of Art! the gem you mould,
> Rich with new taste, with ancient virtue bold,
> Form the poor fetter'd slave on bended knee,
> From Britain's sons imploring to be free;
> Or, with fair Hope the bright'ning scenes improve,
> And cheer the dreary wastes of Sydney Cove;
> Or, bid Mortality rejoice and mourn,
> O'er the fine forms on Portland's mystic urn ;—
> Whether, O Friend of Art! your gems derive
> Fine forms from Greece, and fabled gods revive;
> Or bid from modern life the portrait breathe,
> And bind round Honour's brow the laurel wreath ;—
> Buoyant shall sail, with Fame's historic page,
> Each fair medallion o'er the wrecks of age;
> Nor time shall mar, nor steel, nor fire, nor rust,
> Touch the hard polish of the immortal bust."

Mr. Wedgwood lived long enough to see the Staffordshire Potteries—in his boyhood a series of thinly-populated villages—in a fair way to become, what they now are, a chain of towns and manufactures, in which tens of thousands are constantly employed and supported. He died, universally regretted, in January, 1795, in the sixty-fifth year of his age, and was buried in the parish church of Stoke. A monument is erected there to his memory; but his best memorial is the character which he left behind him, and for which he is still revered in the district.

RENNEQUIN, LAURENS, HARRISON, GOBELIN, GED, AND OTHERS.

In this chapter are given a few short notices of men whose labours deserve mention, and most of whom were only deterred from producing greater results by the want of those aids which are now communicated to workmen of every grade, down to the most humble.

ONE of the greatest mechanical inventions of the time of Louis XIV. was the celebrated Marly machine, constructed for the purpose of raising the waters of the river Seine to the top of the Marly Mountain, and thence conveying them to Versailles. This admirable work was designed by a humble carpenter of Liege, named Swalm Rennequin, born in 1644. He followed the trade of his father, and was so entirely uneducated that he could not even read. He possessed, however, a truly wonderful genius for mechanics, and early showed skill in the invention of machinery; his attention being particularly directed to the subject of under-drainage, so important for the working of the mines and pits which abound in the Liegois territory.

When Louis XIV. had built the Château de Versailles, it was found necessary to devise some means for the supply of water, of which there was a deficiency. The royal minister, Colbert, by the command of the monarch, turned his attention to the matter, and in the course of his inquiries applied to the Chevalier Deville, who was a landed proprietor, and owner of a château where Rennequin had been employed by him to construct a machine for raising water, which was of a similar description to that of Marly, and of which, it is said, some vestiges still remain. Deville went to Paris, accompanied by Rennequin, who formed his project and made some preliminary experiments, which proved sufficiently satisfactory to the Court, and the vast undertaking was commenced in 1675, and brought to a close in 1682. It is said to have cost above four millions of pounds sterling, and by its complicated machinery and many excellent contrivances, excited general surprise and admiration. It did not, however, raise all the water it might have done, because the maker was unacquainted with certain principles of mathematical science by which his inventive skill would have been seconded and rendered far more successful.

It awakens one's interest to learn that Rennequin's merit as the original inventor of this great work was disputed. M. Prony, his biographer, says that a portrait of Deville was engraved, bearing an inscription which ascribed the honour to him; but it is beyond question that he was merely the negotiator of the enterprise with the Minister and the Court. Professor Weidler, who was contemporary with Rennequin, and who visited and described his machine, says positively that he learned, on strict investigation, the humble and modest mechanic was the sole originator and maker of it.

"Let him who earned it, bear the palm!"

What far greater works would this man have effected had he enjoyed those helps which his successors have had!

Another mechanician deservedly celebrated for the skilful application of his art to the science of hydraulics, was Laurens, the son of a sluice-keeper of Bouchain, whose success was the more remarkable because he also was almost entirely without education. He drained marshes in Flanders and Hainault which had been abandoned as impracticable, facilitated the navigation of the Scarpe, and constructed sluices in other rivers. The junction of the Escaut and the Somme presented seemingly insurmountable difficulties, but Laurens determined to master them, and he succeeded; effecting his purpose by means of a subterranean canal, three leagues in length, which united with the Escaut forty-five feet above its source, and with the Somme fifteen feet below its level.

Who has not heard of the celebrated Gobelin tapestry? Perhaps few are aware of the origin of the name, or have heard of the brothers Gobelin, who, in the reign of Francis I., introduced from Venice into France the art of dyeing scarlet, and established, for that purpose, extensive workshops upon the small river Bièvre, which bathes the southern extremity of the faubourg St. Marceau, in Paris. In the fourteenth century the waters of this brook were considered excellent for dyeing. Numerous drapers and dyers established themselves upon its banks, their houses and bleach-grounds presenting a pleasant and picturesque aspect, whilst the waters ran of every colour of the rainbow, resembling various strata of differently-coloured minerals. Here, in 1450, Jean Gobelin erected a modest dwelling, and commenced his operations. His project was considered at the time, by the rival dyers of the metropolis, so hazardous that it was called "Gobelin's Folly;" but, undismayed by their ridicule, the Venetian continued to dye his scarlet, and by the brilliancy and permanence of the colours he produced, he soon commanded the admiration of his fellow-mechanics, and the Parisians were astonished to such a degree that they said Gobelin had made a compact with the devil!

Fashion soon smiled propitiously upon the labours of his skill and industry; and he who had once knelt on the ground and washed the cloth in the waters of the Bièvre with his own hands, now grew rich apace. His sales were rapid, orders poured in upon him from distant places, and he became the master of numerous workmen, whom, to his honour it is said, he treated with so much consideration and liberality that they looked upon him as their friend. After his death the business was carried on successfully by his family; and in the year 1677, Colbert, the great minister of Louis XIV., purchased the dyehouses from the then proprietors, and established on the ground a great manufactory of tapestry, similar to that of Flanders. The celebrated Lebrun was appointed director-in-chief of the establishment; and under his administration were fabricated those splendid tapestries which have since been the admiration of the world, comprising Alexander's battles, the Four Seasons, the Elements, and the principal events in the reign of Louis XIV.

Allusion has already been made* to the celebrated John Harrison, who may fairly be regarded as the parent of modern chronometry. This remarkable man was one of those who had to struggle against the disadvantages of an inadequate knowledge on the subjects connected with his favourite pursuits; and so many were the difficulties in his way, that more than forty years were spent in perfecting his admirable improvements in the construction of timekeepers, and bringing them into use.

He was the son of a carpenter, and was born at Foulby, in Yorkshire, in the year 1693. His father, who could not afford to give him a good education, employed him, as soon as he was able to work, in his own business, and occasionally, as was usual with country mechanics, in land-surveying and repairing clocks and watches. A touching incident is related of his childhood. When he was only six years old he suffered from that terrible malady the small-pox, and his parents found that the most efficacious mode of diverting his thoughts from the tedium and pain he endured was to allow him to examine the movements

* See p. 70, note

of a watch, which was placed for that purpose, open, upon his pillow.

The family removed, in 1700, to Barrow, in Lincolnshire, where the clergyman of the place, noticing the boy's genius for mechanical pursuits, lent him a MS. copy of Professor Saunderson's lectures, which he carefully and neatly transcribed. It may be readily imagined how valuable such scientific aid proved to the young student, and how diligently he turned it to account.

It was not before 1725 that he had so far surmounted the difficulties of his situation as to have constructed two clocks, chiefly of wood, to which he had applied the escapement and compound-pendulum of his own invention, the excellence of which depended upon the different degrees in which metals are expanded or contracted by variations of temperature. This important principle is now employed in the construction of the balance-wheels of chronometers, and is that on which the accuracy of these timekeepers mainly depends. These pieces of workmanship surpassed everything of the kind previously made, scarcely varying a second in a month. Encouraged by his success, Harrison took his clocks to London, and showed them to Halley, Graham, and others, who gave him certificates of their merit, and advised him to perfect his inventions. He accordingly returned home and completed his timekeeper, which fully answered his expectations in a long trial, during much bad weather, and subject to the motions of a vessel, on the river Humber

In the year 1736 he again went to the metropolis, and was sent by the Board of Longitude to Lisbon, to make trial of its properties. In this voyage he succeeded in correcting the dead reckoning nearly a degree and a half. From that time he went on improving his invention, until at length he received the whole of the promised reward—£20,000. He died in the year 1776, having nearly completed his eighty-third year. It is said that he could converse with precision and great clearness on mechanics and topics connected with that science; but his want of education rendered it very difficult for him to explain his meaning in writing; he was, in fact, says Mr. Watt, "utterly unqualified to explain by his publications his own notions or inventions."

The art of stereotype-printing has of late years come very much into use, and is a remarkable illustration of the tendency of some inventions to return, after a long course of improvement, very nearly to their original simplicity. The first attempts at printing were, in fact, stereotypes, made with solid plates, on which all the characters in a page were impressed in relief. At the present day the term is only applied to impressions made with plates of fixed type metal, upon pages composed of ordinary characters, or those engraved upon copper in intaglio.

The history of the modern stereotype is somewhat obscure; and different accounts are given of the various projects which bear an affinity to the art. One of the earliest schemes was invented by a Dutchman named Vander Mey, who lived at Leyden, about the end of the sixteenth century. With the assistance of Müller, the clergyman of the German congregation there, he prepared and cast the plates for a quarto Bible, which, after being set up in the usual way, were converted into a solid mass by soldering them together at the back. This method of preparing solid blocks fell into disuse after the death of the inventor, being very expensive, and only applicable to rare cases.

One of the first, if not absolutely the first, to practise stereotyping, according to the common acceptation of the word, was William Ged, a goldsmith of Edinburgh. His claim to this honour is recorded in a rare pamphlet, published by Nichols, in 1781, entitled "Biographical Memoirs of W. Ged, including a particular account of his progress in the art of block-printing." From this work we learn that about the year 1725 Ged invented a process for casting whole pages, and that a few years later he and others associated with him in partnership endeavoured to apply his invention to the printing of Bibles and Prayer-books, for which a privilege was obtained from the University of Cambridge. It is much to be lamented that these ingenious and meritorious efforts were thwarted by the prejudice and opposition of the compositors. One of the people intrusted with the secret avowed that all the books printed in stereotype had been made incorrect, purposely to bring them into discredit. In consequence of this nefarious conduct they were suppressed at the University, and most of the plates destroyed. "After much ill usage," says Mr. Tilloch, "Ged, who appears to have been a person of great honesty and simplicity, returned to Edinburgh. His friends were anxious that a specimen of his art should be published, which was done by subscription. His son James, who had been apprenticed to a printer, with the consent of his master, set up the forms in the night-time, when the other compositors were gone home, for his father to cast the plates from; by which means his edition of Sallust was finished in 1739. This is the first known essay in stereotype-printing. Another work was also printed from plates manufactured by Ged. This was the well-known book entitled "The Life of God in the Soul of Man," which has the following imprint:—"Newcastle: printed and sold by J. White, from plates made by Wm. Ged, goldsmith in Edinburgh, 1742."

Ged's knowledge of the art may be said to have died with his son, whose proposals for reviving it (published in 1751) not having met with encouragement, he went to Jamaica, where he died.

Surely the man who, though unsuccessful in his career, invented the art which has since been carried on with so much success both in Britain and France, deserves to be ranked among the worthies of his class, and should not be forgotten, nor the merit of his invention ascribed to others. How many more examples of genius struggling against difficulties and unbefriended by patronage might be added; but for the present these must suffice.

It has already been said that diligent occupation in the pursuit of business and trade is no obstruction to the development of intellectual life, as is apparent from the fact that many who have attained to high distinction in physical and literary science have sprung from the class of working men. The history of these men does not properly come within the compass of this little book, yet it is hardly to be doubted that the incidents of their lives would offer much of interest to the reader.

BEZALEEL—HIRAM—PAUL.

It seems to me that I cannot more appropriately close this little book than by devoting a few pages to the three illustrious workmen of the Bible whose names you read above. The first was the principal artisan employed about the furniture of the Tabernacle; the second King Solomon's chosen superintendent for the work of the Temple, and the third the great prototype of all Christian workmen.

If we would know the true excellence of labour and the high value which God sets upon it, we must search the pages of Scripture, which are indeed a record, from their commencement to their close, of work, divine and human, spiritual, moral, and manual.

Who that reads the "Book of the Law" but must at once be struck with the precise details given of the workmanship of the Ark and furniture of the Tabernacle. When God saw fit to have "ordinances of divine things and a worldly sanctuary," He made known to His servant Moses His will respecting all things, down to the minutest particular, and the work was to be done after a given pattern, which was shown him in the Mount.

Then Moses brought his message to the Israelites, and said, "This is the thing which the Lord hath commanded." There was work to be done, and it must be wrought "with a willing heart." And the people were favourably disposed, and contributed materials for the construction of the Tabernacle and its furniture. The men brought abundance of stores, nor were the women behind with their gifts. Such of them as were "wise-hearted" spun with their hands, and all things were soon ready. Then Moses came forward and said, "See, the Lord hath called by name Bezaleel, the son of Uri, the son of Hur, of the tribe of Judah, and He hath filled him with the spirit of God, in wisdom, in understanding, and in knowledge, and in all manner of workmanship."

The skilful artificer thus divinely indicated was immediately constituted superintendent of the work, and he was endowed with wisdom to teach others; beside which, an assistant was appointed to him, named Aholiab.

Bezaleel means "in the shadow of God;" and this appellation seems to indicate piety in his parents. He was probably the son of a devout Jew, whose name, as well as that of his father, has been preserved to us in consequence of the superior skill and high distinction attained by his illustrious offspring.

What an eventful life must Bezaleel have led from his youth upwards! He probably had practised his craft in Egypt; and may, perchance, have had a hand in carving some of these marvellous monuments of art that yet survive, in ruins, there. One can fancy his chisel working upon the capitals of a grand temple or tomb, whose vestiges lie buried now beneath the sands of that wonderful land. But he was not always to work in Egypt; the summons came for the Israelites to leave the house of bondage, and Uri and Bezaleel, and all their household, fled before the wrath of Pharaoh; their eyes saw the wonders wrought at the Red Sea, and their feet trod the mysterious pathway opened by the waves. But a few months had elapsed since that glorious Exodus, and now, in the wilderness of Sinai, the chosen people awaited the commands of Heaven.

How must Bezaleel have felt when he heard his name uttered by the great leader of his nation! How, conscious of a power hitherto unknown, the inspiration of the Holy Spirit, he stood erect, and advancing at the summons, waited to receive from Moses the requisite instructions for the work he had to do.

In the 36th, 37th, 38th, and 39th chapters of Exodus the details are given of the making of the Tabernacle and its furniture, and at the close it is said, "Bezaleel, the son of Uri, the son of Hur, of the tribe of Judah, made all that the Lord commanded Moses, and with him Aholiab, son of Ahisamach, of the tribe of Dan, an engraver and a cunning workman; an embroiderer in blue, purple, scarlet, and fine linen."

Bezaleel then rested from his work, and we hear no more of him; but of the things he wrought much more is recorded, both in sacred and secular history. The candlestick, the table, the golden censer, and the ark of the covenant, with the cherubims of glory overshadowing the mercy-seat;—these works of beauty, of mystery, and of immortal fame, who has not heard of them? who has not longed to see them? They were, indeed, the shadows and the types of heavenly things. Wondrous works these, wrought by Bezaleel; illustrious workman he, and all honour his, throughout the generations of Israel!

Of *Hiram* we find mention made in 1st Kings, 7th chapter. King Solomon, "in all his glory," was seated on the throne of Israel; his heart within him devising great things, and his zeal burning for the glory of the God of his fathers. He was about to build the temple, which his father David had purposed to erect, but was commanded to abstain, and to depute the work to his son. With his dying breath he had said to Solomon, "Build thou the sanctuary of the Lord God, to bring the ark of the covenant of the Lord and the holy vessels of God into the house that is to be built to the name of the Lord." And now the time was come for the youthful and brilliant monarch to execute the task. The design or pattern of the sacred edifice was with him; David had given it him; and all the stores of precious metals necessary, with the stone and timber, the iron and brass—which the great servant of God had prepared, as he so touchingly said, "in his trouble," for the house of his God,—were ready to hand. There were also workmen in abundance, "hewers and workers of stone, and timber, and all manner of cunning men for every manner of work."

Nothing was wanting save a master mind—a man of consummate skill and energy, to take the superintendence and direct the whole. It appears that none such was to be found in Jerusalem or in Israel; for Solomon applied to the king of Tyre, who, in addition to timber from the forests of Lebanon, and provisions of various kinds, furnished him with the man he needed, a first-rate workman of his late father's. In a letter, which is quite a model of courtesy and generous feeling, he expressed his sympathy in the great undertaking his brother monarch was about to accomplish, and said that he had found for him a "cunning man, endued with prudence and understanding."

This man was *Hiram*, the son of a Tyrian father and a Jewish mother, who was an admirable artificer in brass or copper. Not that his skill was confined to this branch of art, for he wrought also in gold and silver, and in iron, stone, and timber, and could grave any manner of graving; beside which he was an adept in the curious embroidery which was so much in request for the hangings and curtains of the holy places of the Israelites, and also for the vestments of the priesthood, "for glory and for beauty."

Gladly did Solomon send and fetch this renowned artisan out of Tyre; and he, with willing mind, came to the king, and engaged to do all his work, according to the directions given to him. In the 1st Kings, chap. vii., and in 2nd Chron., chaps. iii. and iv., particular mention is made of all he wrought, and at the close it is said, "So Hiram made an end of doing all the work that he made for King Solomon, for the house of the Lord."

His principal works, the masterpieces of his skill, were the two pillars for the porch of the Temple, with their elaborate and exquisite ornaments; and the huge molten sea of brass, supported upon twelve oxen, with its curiously-edged brim, "wrought like the brim of a cup, with flowers of lilies." Numerous other of his minor productions are also specified.

Undoubtedly Hiram, as a skilful and accomplished artisan among the Jews, has no equal save Bezaleel. His name and the memorial of his works have attained immortal renown; nor should it be forgotten that to have ranked first among the workmen of Tyre was to be as a king among princes; as we may learn from the eloquent apostrophe to that great merchant city, *in the 27th chapter of the prophet Ezekiel.*

We have now to consider the great exemplar of the Christian workman; the man who, in a pre-eminent degree, presents a model worthy the imitation of all who aspire to render the work of their hands a service of the heart. This man, the great Apostle of the Gentiles, was called, before his conversion to Christianity, Saul.

He was a Jew, born in Tarsus, then the chief city of Cilicia, and was lineally descended from the patriarch Abraham, of the tribe of Benjamin. The place of his birth was celebrated for polite learning, and, in all probability, he was educated in Greek literature, as we find him subsequently giving proof of his acquaintance with several of the Greek poets. He himself has told us that he was brought up in Jerusalem, "at the feet of Gamaliel," that is to say, he received the instructions of that celebrated Jewish Rabbi, under whom he made great proficiency in the study of the law and the traditions so much esteemed by the Hebrews. This did not, however, prevent him from learning a useful trade it appears to have been customary among the Jews, even in the case of such as had a better education than ordinary, to acquire some business by which they might be enabled, in case of need, to support themselves by honest industry. And thus did Saul of Tarsus. The learned and zealous student of the law was also a skilful and industrious mechanic. While his natural abilities qualified him to aspire to excellence in all departments of knowledge, his laudable independence, which would not suffer him to be chargeable to any man, made it desirable that he should be a good workman. And none can doubt that whatever this man did was well done, and that whatsoever his hand found to do, he did it with his might.

As we have seen, Bezaleel and Hiram put forth the highest efforts of their skill for a glorious service. To prepare a shelter for the Ark of God, and a sanctuary for Divine worship during the wanderings of the favoured nation; to raise a Temple on Mount Zion for the Holy One, which He might delight to honour with the tokens of His presence;—these were high and lofty aims for the devout workmen of the Old Dispensation.

But the Christian Church made no such requirements: instead of a temple made with hands, it pointed the eye of faith to one, eternal in the skies, and in place of the gorgeous services of the Israelitish ritual, it substituted the sacrifices of a broken and a contrite heart. No vestments embroidered with gold and scarlet were required to adorn "the great High Priest" of the Gospel. He had "passed into the heavens," having, once for all, made atonement by His own blood, for the sins of the world.

How, then, might the servant of Christ best consecrate his manual labour, as well as all the efforts of his mind and heart to the service of his God and Saviour? Hear his own touching language, when taking his leave of the elders of the Ephesian church. After appealing to them as witnesses of his trials, his labours, and his fervent love toward them, he concludes by saying, "I have coveted no man's silver, or gold, or apparel; yea, ye yourselves know that these hands have ministered to my necessities, and to them that were with me. I have showed you all things; how that, so labouring, ye ought to support the weak, and to remember the words of the Lord Jesus, how He said, 'It is more blessed to give than to receive.'"

This was the high, disinterested, and noble end of the apostle's labour. He would not even exact his righteous claims from those to whom he ministered in spiritual things, but worked "with labour and travail, night and day," at his occupation,—which was that of a tent-maker,—that he might procure the means of relieving the wants of his poorer brethren, his companions in the faith and patience of the Gospel. The Christain workman had attained his high aim when the labour of his hands had thus been consecrated.

"This is indeed admirable and heroic conduct," some young man who reads this page may say; "to labour thus for other people, and to deny himself both rest and recreation in order to do so, was noble; but, I confess, I don't feel that I have it in me to go and do the like." No! my ingenuous reader, it is not in you, by nature; nor was it in Saul of Tarsus, till it pleased God to call him by His grace. So far from labouring night and day to support the necessitous; he employed his leisure hours in persecuting, with blind zeal, the followers of Jesus of Nazareth. But no sooner had the heavenly vision appeared to him, when on his way to Damascus, and arrested him in his career, than Saul the persecutor was transformed into Paul the apostle. Then a new principle was born within him; the power of Divine Love was felt in his soul, and from that time forward his life was spent in doing God and man service.

According to the Saviour's own words—"Except a man be born again, he cannot see the kingdom of God." But, when once this great transition is wrought within him, he asks, "Lord, what wilt Thou have me to do?" for he feels that he must live no longer unto himself, but unto Him that so loved him as to die for him.

What honour have all they that serve Christ!

Amid the toils of their daily labour they have communion with God; and, when prosperous in all the works of their hands, they joyfully present to Him the sacrifices of praise and thanksgiving which are acceptable through Jesus Christ. "Diligent in business, fervent in spirit, serving the Lord," is their motto; and He Himself is their exceeding great reward. Reader! this shall be your happiness if the Lord be your God. Render to Him the service of your life, then will He bless you, "in all that you set your hands to," and, in the great Day of final account, will pronounce you

"A Workman needing not to be ashamed."

THE END.

CPSIA information can be obtained
at www.ICGtesting.com
Printed in the USA
LVHW111756190123
737431LV00008B/688

9 783375 134242